Love is
a time of enchantment:
in it all days are fair and all fields
green. Youth is blest by it,
old age made benign: the eyes of love see
roses blooming in December,
and sunshine through rain. Verily
is the time of true-love
a time of enchantment—and
Oh! how eager is woman
to be bewitched!

THE INHERITANCE

Mary Ellen Christian, along with six relatives she has never met, has inherited a fortune from a distant cousin, Ralph Dartmoor, who has died. They have also inherited Ralph's old house, isolated on the bleak, rugged New England coast. When Mary Ellen chooses to live in the house and restore it, a host of bizarre things happen, and, one by one, her relatives are mysteriously killed. What else has she inherited in this atmosphere tense with fear and trembling?

Books by Daoma Winston
in the Ulverscroft Large Print Series:

THE SECRETS OF CROMWELL CROSSING
SINISTER STONE
THE INHERITANCE

DAOMA WINSTON

THE INHERITANCE

Complete and Unabridged

ULVERSCROFT
Leicester

This edition first published in Great Britain in 1987 by
Judy Piatkus (Publishers) Ltd.,
London

First Large Print Edition
published January 1989
by arrangement with
Judy Piatkus (Publishers) Ltd.,
London

British Library CIP Data

Winston, Daoma, *1922–*
The inheritance.—Large print ed.—
Ulverscroft large print series: romance, suspense
I. Title
813′.54[F]

ISBN 0-7089-1986-3

Published by
F. A. Thorpe (Publishing) Ltd.
Anstey, Leicestershire
Set by Rowland Phototypesetting Ltd.
Bury St. Edmunds, Suffolk
Printed and bound in Great Britain by
T. J. Press (Padstow) Ltd., Padstow, Cornwall

FOR
Ruth and Mike Mosettig

1

IT would have been almost funny if it hadn't hurt so much.

Mrs. George was waiting just inside the door. She had a dust rag in her hand, as if I had surprised her in the midst of giving one more unnecessary polish to the cabinet of small knickknacks in the hallway.

I had known she would be there. That was what was almost funny.

It hurt because I knew she was afraid.

When I let myself in, her small round filmy eyes anxiously searched my face, and her white head tipped toward me.

I consciously straightened my shoulders and pasted a determined smile on my lips. "Hi," I said, with all the cheer I could muster. "Why don't you leave that for me? I'll do it as soon as I change my clothes."

Her wrinkled lips pursed and trembled over the unasked question and the unspoken answer that lay between us.

I saw her struggle and felt ashamed. I

knew how worried she was, and I knew why.

I said gently, "No, Mrs. George, I didn't get the job."

She blinked, and her wren-thin body pressed hard against the wall. She whispered, "But Mary Ellen. What are you going to do? What are *we* going to do?"

We had been through this frightened little scene so many times in the past three months that I had been able to predict it ahead of time.

It always began very early when, carefully dressed, brushed, my heart high with hope, I set out on an interview. Mrs. George would be up, smiling happily, to wish me luck, to say, "This is it, Mary Ellen. I know. I can feel it. Today you'll find a place." I would agree and promise to come straight back to share the good news with her. And then the job wouldn't materialize. I would be so sure that it would, but something would happen. I would return with bad news instead of good. Mrs. George would be waiting hopefully, and I would try to smile. But I would understand her growing fear.

2

She was a widow, her only son dead in the war and buried with full military honors at Arlington National Cemetery. All she had was a small pension, and the tiny cottage in which she lived. The rent I paid for my room augmented her impossibly inadequate income. Without it she couldn't manage. Much as she wanted to, she couldn't let me stay on without paying her. My own savings had dwindled to almost nothing. I would have to move within a few weeks.

In the three months since I had rented the room from her we had become friends, even though she was in her mid-seventies and I was only twenty-two. Perhaps my experience as companion to old Kelly Galligher had helped to establish this easy relationship between us, though pert, quick, warm-hearted Gina George was very different indeed from crusty, moody Kelly Galligher.

I didn't want to allow my thoughts to dwell on him. His sudden death, just before I moved in with Mrs. George, had been a painful shock to me, and I had been shaken to my very soul by what had happened afterward.

Mrs. George's warmth had been a kind antidote to the poison of those memories, and I was grateful that she allowed me to do some of the small chores around the cottage and permitted me to feel at home as I had felt nowhere else in my whole life.

But now she repeated worriedly, "Mary Ellen, what are we going to do?"

I patted her thin shoulder. I broadened my smile with an effort that made my face ache. "Why, we'll manage. Something will turn up."

I didn't tell her that I had reached a decision. I didn't yet know what I would do, or where I would go. But when I no longer had the rent money, I would make sure that she had a roomer to take my place and then, knowing I had to, I would leave.

She gave me a smile as false as mine had been. "Yes," she agreed. "Something will surely turn up, won't it?" And then, "I know. We'll have us a nice cup of tea. A cup of tea always helps, doesn't it, Mary Ellen?"

"That would be wonderful," I said to please her.

She tucked the dust rag into the pocket of her red apron and hurried off to the kitchen.

I had started down the hall to my room when I heard her cry, "Oh, Mary Ellen. Oh, my goodness! I forgot! I forgot all about it! And it might be important. Mary Ellen! Look! Look here what came for you while you were out!"

I turned back.

She stood in the doorway, waving a long white envelope. Her wrinkled face was flushed with annoyance at herself. I knew she felt that she shouldn't be susceptible even to very natural forgetfulness.

"It's probably just an ad," I grinned. But I felt a quick lift of hope just the same. Perhaps one of those prospective jobs that had fallen through was about to materialize after all. When I took the long white envelope from Mrs. George's trembling hand I knew that she was thinking just the same thing.

I was touched at her concern. I knew that she wasn't worried just for herself, for her rent. She was worried about me, too. I winked at her, then glanced down at the envelope.

It was of thick, cream-colored parchment, a heavy and expensive paper. The return address was embossed in sharp black print. It read, *Gentry Carrier, Attorney at Law*, and gave an address in the city.

Mrs. George was waiting, her expectant eyes fixed on my face.

"I don't think it's an ad," I told her.

"Then open it, Mary Ellen. See what's inside."

I was strangely reluctant. I didn't know why. I looked at the return address again. "It's from a lawyer."

"A lawyer? Oh, dear." Mrs. George backed into the kitchen. She sank down on a chair, her wrinkled face suddenly full of anxiety. "A lawyer. . . ."

I took a deep breath, wondering if somehow those terrible moments after Kelly Galligher's death were about to become real again—if the swift horror that had engulfed me then was about to engulf me once more. I slid a finger under the envelope flap, opened it carefully. Carefully I drew out the heavy sheet. I read it quickly, my disbelief growing with each

6

sentence, and then I looked up at Mrs. George.

She waited, not wanting to ask, but willing me with her anxious eyes to tell her.

I let my fingers curl around the letter, the thick paper crumpling between them. "It's crazy," I said, "and impossible. It has to be a mistake."

She blinked. Her wrinkled lips pursed. She got to her feet. "You'd better sit down, Mary Ellen. Do you know you're as white as a ghost?"

I felt as white as a ghost, and weak-legged, all my muscles turned to water. I lowered myself into a chair gingerly, grateful for its solid support. "But it must be a mistake, you see." I pushed the letter toward her. "It says I've inherited something. A bequest of substantial value. Though I don't know just what. And that's absolutely impossible. He must mean someone else by the same name. I don't have any relatives. I never have had."

Mrs. George took the crumpled letter and smoothed it. She studied it carefully, her pursed lips moving as she read each sentence twice. Finally she shook

7

her head. "But it says you, Mary Ellen. You see? Right here. It says Mary Ellen Christian. And that's you." She leaned back, laughing merrily. "That's wonderful, my dear. You're an heiress! You go and talk to him and you'll see. Everything is all right now. We don't have to worry any more."

I wouldn't let myself believe it. I couldn't. I didn't dare. I knew it had to be a mistake. I said, "But there's no one to leave me anything, Mrs. George. You know that just as well as I do. I've told you that I never knew my mother or father. I never had any family."

She bustled to the stove, banged the tea kettle on, lit the flame under it. She thrust bread into the toaster, and set out small pots of strawberry and blackberry jam. She took from her best set of china two cups, two saucers, and two cake plates. We were about to celebrate in her favorite way. When she had arranged everything just so, she returned to the table.

She sat opposite me, her eyes fixed on my face. "Mary Ellen, whether you knew them or not, you had parents, and grand-parents. And maybe you had uncles and aunts, too. Somewhere, sometime, there were all those relatives. And if life took you away from them, it was their loss as well as yours. You must remember that. You must remember that the Lord moves in mysterious ways, and perhaps He moved someone, among all your unknown relatives, to remember you before he died."

I nodded slowly. "Maybe, just maybe, you're right, Mrs. George."

"I am. Of course I am." The kettle whistled, and she jumped up and hurried to attend to it, smoothing her red apron. She poured the water, steeping the tea according to her lifelong ritual.

Meanwhile I read the letter once again. It was rather vaguely worded, I realized now. It said only that I had received an inheritance, and that Gentry Carrier would be grateful if I would appear in person at his office to discuss the matter further. It suggested that the letter in hand would be considered appropriate identification, and it should therefore be brought with me when I appeared. The date suggested was two days away. The wording was formal and polite, but it was plainly a summons in the guise of an invitation.

Mrs. George served our tea and toast, smiling happily. "What will you do?" she asked.

"Do?"

"I mean when you have it. When it comes through," she explained. And she added, at my blank look, "Oh, Mary Ellen! The inheritance. I mean the inheritance, of course."

I felt a queer shiver of apprehension. I knew that I mustn't allow myself to believe too much, to hope too much. I said, "I don't know. I'll have to see. I'm still not at all sure. . . ."

"You *are* Mary Ellen Christian," she said firmly.

"Yes. Of course. But just the same. . . ."

"No, Mary Ellen. Stop it. You must have faith."

"It just doesn't seem real to me," I answered. "It doesn't seem possible."

She sat very still, her tiny hand curled around the steaming cup. "You're afraid," she said thoughtfully. "That's what it is, isn't it? You're just afraid to believe that it's true."

I nodded wordlessly.

So much had gone wrong in the past three months. I had begun to feel that nothing would ever go right again.

I was afraid to allow myself to count too heavily on what might be nothing.

The inheritance, if there really was one, even if small, could make all the difference to me. I could stay on with Mrs. George. I could count, perhaps, on enough time in which to find a job. And, once I was working again, I could learn to forget those terrible moments after Kelly Galligher's death, and learn to relinquish my feeling of irretrievable loss.

"I don't know," Mrs. George sighed. "I just don't understand. You're young. You have your whole life ahead of you . . ."

I raised my eyes to hers.

She went on, ". . . but sometimes, just once in a while, you look so sad, Mary Ellen. A shadow seems to touch you."

"I'm all right, Mrs. George. You mustn't start to worry about me," I said quickly.

"Of course you are," she answered. "I

know that. But I wonder. I can't help wondering. That's all."

I knew that she was remembering what I had told her about my life in the years before we met. There had been very little to recount.

I had been abandoned in a day-care center at the age of three. I remembered neither my mother nor my father. I remembered no home except the institution to which I had been sent by the State Welfare office. I was a small, very nervous child, with straight, mouse-colored hair, and too many freckles, and over-large anxious blue eyes. I spoke only rarely, and then in a whisper. I offered affection to no one. Prospective adopting parents never looked at me twice. At sixteen, still small, very thin, I went to a foster home. I was more an unpaid companion than child in that house. At eighteen, I was on my own, but the experience had stood me in good stead. I earned my living as a companion, in several different places, from then on. And then, only nine months before, although it seemed much longer to me, I had met Kelly Galligher.

I had finished my job with Mrs. Alice Delaner, had helped her pack, and had overseen her move to a senior citizen home. I decided I would take a few days off before trying to find a new position. I was feeling the sweetness of spring, of being young and lonely, the day I decided to picnic in the city park. I bought a sandwich and a bottle of soda, and settled down in the shade of an old oak tree. I had my lunch, and read for a little while, and daydreamed for much longer. For so much longer that I was startled when the shadows were long and dark and the sun began to set. I was just gathering my things, preparing to leave, when I heard a clatter nearby and a great shouted oath.

I looked up. On the path just a few yards away, there was a wheel chair. An elderly man sat in it, beating big gnarled fists on its arms. A cane lay on the gravel at his feet, and a scatter of books were spread out around him.

I dropped my things and ran to him. "Are you all right?" I asked.

"Sure," he snarled. "Sure, I'm all right. Only I've dropped my gear. And I can't pick it up."

He had sharp blue eyes, a square, lined face. His hair was thick and white, and stood up over his ears like horns from the angry passes he made at it.

I smiled at him. "Well, there are worse things in the world than dropping your gear, aren't there? I'll be glad to get your books together for you."

"And my cane," he said. "That's what I really need. My cane. I can still walk, you know. Just a few steps maybe, but it's walking. Only I've got to have that cane."

I handed it to him gravely, liking the firm pride in his voice and the sharpness in his blue eyes. Then I gathered the rest of his things, and stacked them on the expensive velvet throw that covered his lap. "Okay now?" I asked.

He didn't answer at first. His blue eyes stared me up and down. His brow furrowed. Then, with a visible effort, he said, "I thank you kindly for your help. But don't rush off. Not unless you're too busy to talk to an old man."

I didn't know what we would talk about, but that didn't matter. He was lonely, and I knew about that. "I'm not busy," I told him.

"Then let's go for a walk," he suggested. "That is, let's you go for a walk, and I'll ride along beside you."

That was the first time I saw Kelly Galligher.

I didn't know then that that accidental meeting would change my life forever.

Now Mrs. George brought me back to the present by asking, "Mary Ellen, what are you going to wear when you go to meet the lawyer?"

"I don't know. A skirt, a blouse. I don't think it matters, does it?"

She grinned like a teen-ager. "But you're an heiress now, so it does matter. You want to make a good impression. You want to look right, and feel right. And to feel right you must look right, so. . . ."

I grinned back at her. "But the truth is, I only want to find out what it's about. And who remembered me in his will. And how I was found."

Suddenly sober, she answered, "Of course you do, Mary Ellen. Of course you do."

The next two days dragged by. I did a few small chores for Mrs. George, shopped for her, and sat before the television set with her.

At last it was time for me to keep my appointment at Gentry Carrier's office.

I brushed my hair until it crackled with electricity. Once it had been a nothing mouse brown. Now it was a strong chestnut with sparkling highlights that glowed when it lay smooth and shining on my shoulders. My freckled face had turned creamy and smooth and my wide-apart eyes were a strong aquamarine blue.

I dusted my cheeks and nose with powder, hoping to disguise the faint sheen of nervousness that I saw on them. I etched a pale pink on my lips, and fastened to my ears the tiny pearl drops that Kelly Galligher had given me.

I put on a short black skirt, a crisp white shirt. My black high-heeled pumps shone with a fresh layer of polish.

Mrs. George gave me a toe to top inspection before she nodded her white head. "There you are, my dear. Yes. You look lovely." And then, "Good luck, Mary Ellen. All the good luck in the world to you, no matter how it goes."

I thanked her breathlessly, and hurried out to catch the bus.

I had allowed plenty of time because Gentry Carrier's office was in a section of the city unfamiliar to me, and I didn't know how long it would take to get there. I was somewhat uneasy when I finally found the building. It was a small one, with several "For Rent" signs on the outside door. The windows were dirty and rain streaked. It had been years since the foyer was swept. It was a place that didn't seem to go with the expensive stationery that the lawyer used. My apprehension became stronger. I had to force myself to take the rickety self-service elevator to the third floor. But I did it. There, at the end of a long dim corridor, I saw, on the frosted glass of a door, gold lettering which said *Gentry Carrier, Attorney at Law.*

For a moment it seemed to glow at me, neon bright and pulsing. It was the stuff of dreams, of hope. My heart yearned toward it. My feet danced.

I held myself still. I breathed slowly and carefully, and counted caution out in silent words. I must not be too disappointed, no matter what happened. I might be the wrong Mary Ellen Christian. Then, with slow and measured step, I went down the corridor.

I paused at the frosted door. I slipped off my white cotton gloves, then pulled them on again.

From within, there was a murmur of voices, cross currents of sound that were infinitely frightening.

Behind me the elevator rattled and hummed away.

I gently turned the knob on the frosted door, and pulled it open.

The murmur of voices instantly stopped.

Six heads turned. Six pairs of eyes stared at me.

I sank in terror and fought to resurface. I wouldn't allow myself to turn, to run away. I had come this far and I would stay and learn what the letter from Gentry Carrier meant.

Clinging tightly to my shaken composure, I crossed the dank brown moth-eaten rug, and took the last vacant chair.

From the corner, a small plump

dimpled blonde, wearing a red mini skirt and black patent-leather sandals with lacings to her round knees, stared at me. Finally, with an arch of made-up brows, she said, "You must be the seventh one. The one we're all waiting for."

2

THE others nodded, silent speculative stares raking me up and down.

The plump dimpled blonde crossed her ankles, and giggled breathlessly, "Well, I don't know about the rest of them, but I'm sure glad you're here. I don't think I could have waited another minute. Not another single minute. And that's what he said. We'd have to wait until you got here. The lawyer, I mean. He has to meet with us together. Not individually. It's necessary, he said, to meet with us together." She turned wide expectant blue eyes toward a closed door which I assumed must lead to an inner office. Then, with a sigh, she swung back to me. "I'm Sally Damson. And in case you haven't figured it out yet, I'm pretty excited about the whole thing."

I had been examining the room as I listened to her. The chairs were orange plastic with chrome arms. The sofa was brown.

Two brown formica tables had orange ashtrays. The single window was dirt streaked and undraped. There was something odd about the furnishings that sat on the moth-eaten rug. They looked almost new, and seemed to have been just recently moved into this unkempt place without interest or care. I wondered if Gentry Carrier had just opened his office here.

I dismissed that question to smile at the plump blonde named Sally. I said, "I'm Mary Ellen Christian. I'm sorry if I caused any delay to you."

"Oh, don't worry. You're not late," one of the men answered gruffly. He sat in an orange plastic chair. "This chick," he jerked his head at Sally, "was early. And so were the rest of us. You might say we were on the anxious side, you know? Only now that I think of it, it blows my mind. We waited all these years, didn't we? Then what's another couple of minutes?"

He had very pale blue eyes, the color of watered ink, and a sharp straight nose. He wore a black curly beard, and his hair was brushed straight back off his forehead. It hung all the way to his shoulders. There was a single gold loop in his right ear. He wore very faded blue jeans, and a sleeveless blue shirt under a long fringed leather vest.

I was certain that I had never seen him before in my life, yet for just an instant, I felt a peculiar sense of recognition, of familiarity. Then it was gone.

His eyes met mine in a cold assessing look, while a wide white grin split his beard. "I give you the shivers and shakes, don't I? You're wondering where I fit in, and who I fit in with, and just what I am to you, aren't you?"

That was true enough. He looked like a pirate in his fringed leather vest and black beard and single gold earring. But I didn't feel it necessary to say so. I smiled back at him. "I guess we're all in this together. Whatever *this* is."

Sally said, "He's Barney Gray. We've already introduced ourselves around. We figured out that we must be some kind of cousins. I mean, how else could we all have shared in the same will? If we weren't some kind of cousins?"

There was an eagerness in her voice that made me think she was saying what she wanted to believe. I wondered suddenly if she had been lonely all her life, too.

The tall slender brunette on the sofa glanced at her wrist watch, and then looked at me. Her green eyes had a faintly malicious sparkle as she said thoughtfully, "Wouldn't it be funny if it were a gag? A con job? Just a trick to get us together and sell us encyclopedias?"

"Stop it," Sally cried. And then to me, "She's been going on like that ever since she got here. What I say is, if that's how she feels, then why doesn't she get up and leave? Then there'd just be six of us. And we could divide it, whatever it is, between us. And . . . ."

"The lady has a suspicious mind, maybe," Barney grinned. "But she won't take a chance like that."

Sally ignored him. "She's Anne Lyttle. I don't know why she has to talk like that, and be a kill-joy. Listen, all my life I dreamed of something great like this. I mean, something that would get me out of that big building and away from that switchboard, and believe you me, the first thing I'm going to do is buy me a plane ticket, and I'm flying down to San Juan,

23

and I'm going to start new and fresh. I'm going to start living!"

Anne's lush lips curved in a disbelieving smile. "You're counting your dollars before you have them, Sally. The last time I did that I found I was empty-handed when the time came to pay the bills."

There was a deep cold bitterness in her husky voice, in the shape of her mouth, that suggested she had known disillusion and disappointment often enough to scar her.

The girl next to her, pert, red-headed, with chocolate brown eyes, gave an approving nod. "You're right, Anne. We'd better not bank on something that might fall through." To me, she added, "I'm Hester Fairleigh."

"James Harrow here," a slim, sandy-haired man said from where he slouched in an orange chair. He had a light, very clear voice, and a noticeable English accent that didn't quite ring true. His hands were pale and smooth, and nervously plucked at the crease in his gray trousers, then shifted to fiddle with the knot in his black tie. Having given me his name, he seemed to sink deeper within his chair.

The last man to introduce himself had a plump round face and gray eyes that seemed expressionless behind big steel-framed glasses. He was very nearly bald, a few strands of dark brown hair spread carefully across his shiny scalp. Still he was plainly young. He said in a languid voice, "I'm Timothy Brown, Miss Christian. I'm glad to meet you."

"And he," Sally crowed, "he couldn't care less about what we're to get."

"Oh, it's not that," he objected. "It's just . . ." he turned back to me, laughed deprecatingly, "It's just that they're so anxious, you see. Perhaps you are, too. But I . . . well, it's simply different for me."

"Then why don't you take off?" Sally demanded resentfully. "Who needs you? Just like I said about Anne. One less to divide among is one less."

Timothy ignored her. "My family, the Jordans, our wealth goes back three generations. Our pedigree goes back to the Mayflower. I assure you I have no need at all of whatever our mysterious benefactor left us, but I . . ."

James cut in, "We believe you, old

chap. No need to go through it once again, I assure you."

"Meantime," Anne said in her smooth husky voice, "it is now ten minutes after two. So what's happened to our Mr. Carrier?"

"You did see him?" I asked. "He was here earlier, wasn't he?"

"Oh, sure," Sally told me. "He's in the back office. We saw him go in. That was after he said he'd wait until we were all assembled. I guess maybe he's doing some work or something. Or maybe he doesn't know we're all here yet."

"Then suppose someone knocks and tells him," James suggested.

"You do it." Hester gave him a bright encouraging smile.

He said stiffly, "Barristers are notoriously more amenable to pretty girls, aren't they?"

Hester preened, her chocolate brown eyes alight with appreciation of the compliment. But she remained seated.

The others picked up the discussion, some urging a patient wait, some suggesting immediate action.

I realized that they felt the same as I

26

did. They were each of them terribly anxious to know what was involved, what Gentry Carrier had to tell them. But, at the same time, they were fearful of a disappointment.

Listening to them bicker, I studied them thoughtfully.

How could we be related? I wondered. What strange quirk of fate had brought us together?

Aside from our reactions to the possibility of the inheritance, I could see only one thing that we had in common. We were plainly each of us in our twenties. I suspected that Anne was probably the oldest, twenty-eight or twenty-nine, and James very close to that. I knew that Sally must be just about my own age, and Hester not more than a year older. Timothy, in spite of his nearly-bald head, and Barney, in spite of his beard, were twenty-five, I judged. I couldn't see that the age cluster meant anything in particular. And if we shared some other bond it wasn't apparent to me.

Perhaps that was why I didn't realize then how quickly and deeply our lives would become entwined, and how this first meeting in Gentry Carrier's office would permanently affect each one of us.

"All right," Sally said suddenly. "Maybe the rest of you are cowards, but I'm not." She jumped to her feet. "I'll do it. I'll knock on the door and tell him we're tired of . . ." Her voice stopped. She gave a breathless giggle.

The door to the inner office opened.

The man I knew must be Gentry Carrier spread a slow smile around the group while his bloodshot eyes moved from one to another of us in an obvious head count.

"Good," he said at last. "Very good. We're all assembled now." His voice was deep, gentle, almost stage-like in its caressing warmth. He was tall, well built. He had dark hair, touched with flecks of gray at the temples. His suit was brown, perfectly cut, and very fashionable. He wore two heavy gold rings on his left hand. They gleamed as he ushered us into the inner office with a wave.

I thought that Gentry Carrier himself, and his stationery, seemed to go together. Both expensive-looking, both done up with attention to every detail. And neither of them seemed to belong in this almost shoddy office.

I forgot that in the excitement of the moment, but later on, I was to remember and wonder.

Now he seated us on folding chairs around his big desk, and sat down behind it. He fanned a stack of papers, then brought them together neatly. He leaned back, and folded his hands, and studied us carefully and slowly.

At last Sally burst out, "All right, all right. What's it all about? I don't have the whole day, you know. I've got to get back to work some time, don't I?"

"You aren't the only one," Anne said. "What about me? What about the rest of us?"

Gentry Carrier raised his hand, and his rings gleamed again. "Please. This is an important matter. Let's not waste our time on frivolities. I myself have other engagements."

"Then let's get on with it, old chap," James answered, nervously tugging at his tie.

The lawyer looked at him, glanced down

at one of the papers before him. "You are, I would suppose, James Harrow. Is that right?"

James nodded, his thin face expressionless.

"Of course," Gentry said. His bloodshot eyes made the circle, touching on each of us as he murmured our names to himself.

"Hey, man," Barney demanded, "is that supposed to be black magic. How do you work it out? We didn't identify ourselves to you."

The lawyer smiled faintly. "Your descriptions are noted here."

"But why?" Anne asked quickly, suspiciously. "I don't understand why anybody . . ."

Gentry Carrier sighed, said in his deep warm voice, "My dear Miss Lyttle, all will be explained in due time." He paused. Then, "First the formalities. You did, each of you, bring with you the letter I sent to you, did you not?"

I nodded. So did the others.

"Then may I have them now? It is another means, as are the descriptions, of identifying you to me more surely. And with them, will you kindly provide me, temporarily, of course, with another means of identification? A driver's license will do nicely. Or a Social Security card. Whatever you have that proves you are who you say you are."

"What's the idea?" Timothy demanded. "I don't get it. You know who we are. You have our descriptions already, and you wrote to us."

"I have been instructed by the will," the lawyer answered. "It is necessary to be certain that my letter wasn't intercepted by a person so eager to be a part of this that he is willing to be an impostor to join us." He smiled faintly. "This is a complicated situation. As you will see."

Timothy grumbled, but subsided into silence.

I had my Social Security card in my wallet. I slipped it out, and passed it, along with the letter, to the lawyer. As I leaned closer to him, he gave me a wide smile, and I caught a whiff of a familiar scent. Kelly Galligher had always had a small drink before going to sleep. It was bourbon, amber-colored and bitter. Now I understood Gentry Carrier's bloodshot eyes.

The others gave him their letters, and identification.

Only Barney offered nothing.

Gentry Carrier examined each submission, then returned it to its proper owner. At last he said, "Mr. Gray?"

"Call me Barney, man," Barney retorted. "We're friends, aren't we? Or we're going to be friends."

"I see no identification from you, Barney," the lawyer said gently.

Barney shrugged. "Look, man, I've been traveling, see. I move a lot, and fast and light. I don't have a car, so I don't have a driver's license. I don't have a job. At least not at the moment. So I don't have a Social Security number. And besides, you ought to be able to figure it out from sizing me up. I don't go for numbers. I don't believe in computers, and files, and all that plastic stuff. Me, I'm a free man. I'm me. You got to take my word for it."

Gentry smiled frostily. "We'll see."

"Do I go or stay?" Barney demanded.

"Stay, by all means." The lawyer's stagy smile grew even frostier. "I have other means of verifying your identity. And I shall."

"Be my guest," Barney retorted, a wide smile growing within his black beard.

Gentry folded his hands on the desk. "Now then, we are ready to begin, I believe."

"And about time," Sally complained.

He gave her a cool reproving look. Then he said, "Just about four years ago, a man named Ralph Dartmoor died in the northern part of the state. He lived in a house on a mountain called Point Janeway, just outside a town called Stony Ridge. Do any of you know the place?"

I shook my head, and so did the others.

The lawyer went on. "Dartmoor had no close heirs, but he knew that he had collateral cousins, very distant ones to be sure, with whom he had had no contact, nor his parents before him, it seems. They were scattered, their children unknown. However, he had a sum of money, and a house, and he determined before his death that these collateral cousins must be located, and each of them be given a share of what he had to leave."

"And we're the seven," Sally crowed joyfully.

"You are the seven," the lawyer repeated.

"That's really quite a nice thing to do," James said. "He must have been a good fellow."

Gentry smiled coolly. "Yes, certainly. He was also determined that the state not receive his estate through default of living heirs."

"A man against the Establishment," Barney chuckled. "That sure sounds like my cousin Ralph."

Gentry smiled again. "You two would have appreciated each other perhaps."

"But what is there?" Timothy asked. "A house? Money? What else? And what does it amount to?"

Anne gave him a narrow green look. "I thought you didn't care. You, you're from that rich family, you said. The Jordans, wasn't it? What difference does it make to you?"

"I'm just asking," Timothy retorted. "I have a right to do that don't I?" and his eyes flickered behind his glasses.

Gentry raised his ring-laden hand. "Please. Let's not leave the main point." Then, "A house. Yes. Some money, too.

Each of you will have a seventh share of the house. But there is a complication in that. I'll get to it in a minute. I mentioned money. There will be a check for you all, one every month, a small income, for as long as you live."

There was a silence.

I found myself listening to the quality of it. It mirrored what I myself felt. A sense of disbelief too strong to be put into words. A fear that there was a misunderstanding of some kind.

Who was Ralph Dartmoor? I wondered.

How had he been related to me?

How had the lawyer been able to trace me?

Then James said, "Very good indeed. Now then, what is the complication about the house?"

3

GENTRY sighed. "That's easy enough to explain to you, but I fear it will not be as easy to resolve."

"Get on with it, man," Barney snapped. "It sounds like you're stalling to me. What's the rub? What's the gimmick? What's the catch? Tell us how we end up losers?"

"No one will end up losing," the lawyer told him firmly. "The problem is that you are seven, you see. It is only one house."

"So we sell it, man. Sell out, and take shares. We'll say thanks a lot and go our own ways, and that'll be the end of the problem." Barney sat back, his beard split in a self-satisfied grin.

Gentry answered softly, "Yes, of course. That is the obvious, the logical, thing to do. However, the house is old, very isolated. The town of Stony Ridge is quite dead. Nothing remains of it but a single store and a gasoline station. Point Janeway is simply not salable at the present moment."

"You mean it's worth nothing?" Sally wailed. "You mean we can't get anything out of it? You mean all this fuss is . . . is just . . ."

"It is a house, and therefore worth something," Gentry said firmly. "Worth quite a bit, I should say, if it were to be fixed up, first of all. And then, when the resort areas in the mountains are exploited. . . ." He shrugged. "You'd stand to gain a great deal. But right now, as it stands, not being marketable, it is not an asset."

"Then where does that leave us?" James asked thinly.

"It leaves us with some money coming in every month," Barney said jubilantly, "and also with a house."

"I suggest," the lawyer cut in, "that you seven discuss the matter of the house between you. I suggest that you return here as a group, let us say at the same time tomorrow, to tell me what your ideas are, and what you would like me to do about the house." He got to his feet, glanced at his watch. "And now, if you'll excuse me, I must be in court very soon."

The others rose, talking among themselves.

I looked at Gentry Carrier. He was busy gathering his papers together, stuffing them into a brief case.

I got up, moved close to him. I said in an undertone, "Mr. Carrier, I'm afraid I don't understand. Who is the relative of mine that was originally Ralph Dartmoor's heir? How did you manage to trace me?"

Gentry gave me a blank look.

I was suddenly aware of the tense silence of the others.

I said, "I never knew my parents, you see. I thought, perhaps, if I could figure out . . ."

Gentry stopped me with a wave of his hand. "My dear, you wouldn't know any of the peoples' names. They go back so far, so very far indeed. And in truth," his voice dropped, "it isn't wise to plow up the past, you know. Just be grateful for what you have received, and . . ."

I cut into his stagy whisper. "I am, of course. But it seems so strange. I have no living relatives that I know of. It seems hard to believe that . . ."

"No one among the seven of you has relatives," he told me. "That was noted during the course of the search for each of you. The lines of descent are very tenuous, but I am satisfied that I have located those seven that are the truthful and legal and rightful heirs to what Ralph Dartmoor left behind."

"Nobody has family?" Sally repeated. "Is that what you just said?" she demanded of the lawyer.

He nodded his dark, gray-flecked head. "That is correct. Which is one of the things that made it so difficult to locate you."

"Then what about you, Timothy Brown," she flashed. "You said your family was rich and famous. If you've got a family, then there's a mistake. You know who you are, and you're faking it. You don't belong with us. You . . ."

Gentry cut in, "You must have misunderstood, Miss Damson. Timothy is certainly . . ."

Timothy's round face was flushed. His shiny scalp was flushed under its lacing of thin hair. His eyes gleamed behind his glasses. He mumbled, "I didn't say my family was still alive, did I? I just said they were important and had a lot of money, way back when. And . . ."

"Oh, never mind. If you're in, you're in," she mumbled. "But you have to admit, it did sound funny for a minute. And a cut into six is still better than a cut into seven."

"But it *is* seven, you know," the lawyer said. He moved quickly toward the door. "And now . . ."

We soon found ourselves in the dingy corridor.

At the elevator we broke into two groups. Gentry and Barney and James and Timothy got in together. The door sighed shut, and they were gone.

"A bunch of gentlemen, our cousins," Hester grinned. "How do you like the way they did that?"

Anne shrugged. "It doesn't surprise me. Nothing does."

"Who cares about them anyway?" Sally laughed. "Me, I just wish I'd asked that lawyer when the checks start coming in, and exactly how much they're for."

"And I wish I knew what we could do about the house," Hester answered. "It's probably more important than the monthly check, you know. Property is . . . well, it's solid, and something to hang on to. And money . . ."

"Money gets spent," Sally said thoughtfully.

"The house," Anne said. "Yes. But if we can't sell it and get our money out of it, what good is it to us?"

I listened to them filled with wonderment. None of them seemed concerned with what was important to me. Who was the real source of the legacy? How had I actually become entitled to it?

I cared about the money, the house. I was grateful for my share of them, for what they could do to make my life more secure. But what I cared about even more was the link to my past, my unknown parents.

The elevator returned. The doors sighed open.

The girls got in and I followed them.

As we returned to the first floor, Anne said, "You're awfully quiet, Mary Ellen. What's on your mind?"

"It's the surprise," I told her. "I guess I still don't really believe it."

It didn't seem necessary to me that I explain my questions, my bewilderment, to her. They were my concern, and my problem. Later on, faced with more questions, more bewilderment, faced with fear, I was glad that I hadn't confided in her.

When we reached the first floor, we found that Gentry Carrier had gone.

Barney, waiting for us with James and Timothy, grinned. "You ought to have seen that car he was driving. A Rolls. I kid you not. A Rolls, no less."

I glanced around the rundown hall. A letter on expensive stationery, an expensively-dressed lawyer, a Rolls Royce . . . how odd those qualities seemed, balanced against the poor neighborhood, the decaying building, the rented look of the furniture in the office. I was troubled without knowing exactly why. I had the uneasy feeling that there was more to Gentry and the legacy than any of us knew. I wondered if there was some way I could find out about him. I wished I had someone to ask. If Kelly Galligher had been alive, I could have turned to him. He would have known. He would have told me what to do. But Kelly was dead.

The feeling of irretrievable loss swept me. Momentarily I forgot the others. I was alone. Alone in an empty world.

Then Barney said, "Listen, cousins, let's have lunch together. Let's have a real celebration. What do you say? I mean, we've got to make some hard and fast decisions anyhow, and we ought to get to know each other since we're all related. So let's do it right away. Like we can settle the business and have some fun at the same time."

"There's a small problem," Anne said in her throaty voice. "I have a job to go to, and . . ."

"So have I," Sally interrupted, "but I say to heck with it. I'm not a switchboard operator any more." She giggled. "I just quit."

Hester told her, "Maybe you'd better wait and see. You don't know what's going to happen yet."

"I know," Sally said happily. "I am an heiress, and I'm going to live happily ever after. And nobody's going to stop me."

"Now that chick has the right idea,"

Barney approved. "What do you say? What about it? Do we get our celebration, or don't we?"

His pale blue eyes were on me, asking, prodding, oddly familiar for an instant.

Then I thought of Mrs. George. She would be waiting anxiously in the hall, pretending to dust the knick-knacks in the cabinet, but waiting for me to return, to tell her what had happened at the meeting with Gentry Carrier.

"I'm for it," Hester was saying. "I'll go along with a celebration."

The others chimed their agreement.

"You can back out if you want to," Barney told me. "But if you do, you'll wreck the whole thing. It's one for all, and all for one from now on. That's how it has to be."

I decided I could call Mrs. George from the restaurant, and agreed to go with the others.

The place that Barney led us to was only at the next corner. It was a dim shadowy lounge with sawdust on the floor, and crooked candles set in wine bottles, and blue-and-white checked plastic table covers.

The waitress wore tight green pants and a tight green tank top. She had long blonde hair that fell across her face when she leaned forward to pass us menus.

Barney ordered drinks for all of us, and then sat back, grinning happily. "This is something, isn't it? Like out of the movies. Not out of real life. I mean, you hear about it, and read about it, and watch it on television. But it never happens to you."

"Only it has," Sally chortled.

"There's still the problem of the house," James said quietly. "And how you can split a house into seven pieces is quite beyond my imagination."

"We'll get to it," Barney answered.

The blonde waitress came with the tray of drinks. She distributed them, then took our food orders quickly, and ducked back into the shadows.

When she had gone, Barney raised his glass. "This is to us, cousins. To the inheritance. And to a happy enterprise."

"I'll drink to that," Timothy said, and gave us each a sudden shy grin that made him look very young in spite of his bald head.

"There's a lot we should have asked

him," Hester said thoughtfully. "He didn't give us much time, did he? But with so many questions. . . ."

"None of them matter," James said. "We know what's important, don't we? We'll have some money coming in every month."

"And there's still the house," Anne retorted. "Which is what you just pointed out to us."

He shook his sandy head. "I have no suggestions. I'm sorry. I'm afraid we'll all lose out on that. If the house can't be sold, then we can't get our shares. And that's that."

"Oh, I don't know." Barney grinned at me over his drink. "What about you, quiet Mary Ellen? Any ideas to offer?"

"I'm afraid not," I told him.

He looked at Sally.

"No," she sighed. "Unless maybe we could rent it. I mean, if somebody would rent it from us, then we could divide that into seven, couldn't we?"

"How do you rent a house that nobody wants?" James asked.

"Maybe one of us could rent it from the rest of us," Hester said.

James nodded, looked thoughtfully around the table. "Mary Ellen, what about you?"

I chuckled at the thought. Here I was, jobless, with my savings almost gone, and the promise of a small monthly income all I had to rely on. How could I do that? I said, "I couldn't afford to rent a house, and run it, too. And besides, I don't know anything about Stony Ridge except what Mr. Carrier told us. Where would I work? What would I do?"

"What kind of work do you do?" Anne asked.

I explained, then added, "But I'm at loose ends right now."

"Loose ends?" she asked.

"Nothing has turned up lately," I told her.

James pursued his line of thought. "How about you, Anne?"

She pursed her red lips. "I'm a dancer." She named a club I had never heard of. "But to tell you the truth, I'm just about finished with that. I don't like the life. I don't like the people you meet. I want to move on to something different, but I haven't found anything different yet. And I sure couldn't take on the house."

"Neither could I," James said. "I'm out of work right now. I used to be an accountant. In a bank." He ran a thin nervous finger around his collar, then fiddled with the knot in his tie. "But I . . . well, it got so confining. The people, the hours, the very air. I quit. I guess I'll get something else one of these days."

Hester said pertly, "Don't go looking at me. What would I do in a house by myself? How would I manage? I'm a typist, but I don't much like it." She widened her chocolate brown eyes. "And the boss' wife doesn't much like me, so I won't be surprised if I've been fired for not coming in today."

Barney's rich chuckle covered us like a blanket. His watered-ink blue eyes glowed with hidden embers. "We're a fine bunch, aren't we? I'll bet there's not a one of us who knows what he wants, where he's going. . . ."

"And I suppose you do?" Anne asked acidly.

Barney's rich laugh became an amused bellow. "Me? Me, less than any of you, and I'm not ashamed of it either. I've been doing nothing but drifting for the past five years. I tried everything, and tried nothing, too. Like the more there is the less there is."

"I guess I found soul brothers when I found my cousins," Timothy grinned. "I used to work in a shoe store. I just quit about five minutes ago."

"You! In a shoe store. Timothy Brown, what kind of a liar are you?" Sally cried. "You told us you had a rich family. All about the Jordans. Then you said . . ."

"I know what I said," he retorted. "And it's true, I tell you. It's absolutely true. But they all died, and they lost all their money. And I had to eat. I had to eat just like anybody else, didn't I?"

"You ate too much, judging by your shape," thin James muttered.

Barney said quickly, "You know what I think? I think there's not a single one of us that has ties in this town, nor any reason to hang around here."

"That seems true enough," Anne agreed.

James said something then, but I didn't hear it. I was considering what Barney had just said. None of us had ties in town. We had no ties. We were alone.

I hadn't felt so much that way until Kelly Galligher died.

I had taken for granted my life, my loneliness, until I had those six months with him.

It began the day of my accidental meeting with him in the park. He rode in his wheel chair, and I walked beside him. We exchanged names and brief biographies. We spoke of inconsequentials until it was nearly dark. Then he pushed his wheel chair back toward the road. I was startled to see a long black limousine waiting, and a chauffeur.

Kelly pushed himself to his feet, leaned on his cane. He grinned at the middle-aged man. "Mark, this is Mary Ellen. And Mary Ellen, this is Mark Gormley. He's my driver, and my strong right arm, and my friend. He and his wife Julie keep me going. I want you to get along, because you're going to be spending time together."

Kelly didn't give me a chance to ask why, or how, that would happen. He went on, "Mary Ellen, promise that you'll meet me tomorrow."

There was such urgency in his pale blue eyes, such open hunger, that I couldn't refuse him. I promised I would meet him. He offered to have Mark drive me home, but I refused, saying it was just a few blocks away.

"But you'll be here tomorrow?" Kelly insisted, while Mark waited, impassive, to help him into the limousine.

When I nodded, he leaned on Mark's thick shoulder and clumsily sat down.

Mark folded the velvet throw, collapsed the wheel chair and slid it inside.

Kelly sat watching me, silent, thoughtful, until Mark drove away.

The next afternoon when I got there, he was already waiting. Mark stood with him, his lined face impassive.

Kelly said, "I want you to come to my house for lunch, Mary Ellen."

"But I brought lunch for both of us," I protested.

"Then we'll eat here first, and go later," he said, and then asked Mark to return for us in an hour. When we were alone, he said, "Mary Ellen, I've been thinking about you all night. I guess you're an answer to an old man's prayer. I need help. I need somebody but not a nurse, you understand. That's the thing. I'm not sick. I don't want a snippy thing in white saying, 'Now let's have our bath,' and 'let's go to bed,' and know that's not what she means at all." He grinned, then went on, his voice gruff. "What I need is somebody like you. To pick up my cane for me when I drop it. And ignore my language when it turns blue. And let me holler at you if I have to. And read to me, or listen to me complain. Do you think you can stand it?" I was so taken aback I could hardly answer. It was a coincidence that I was free, that my job with Mrs. Delaner had just come to an end. He demanded, "Well, well? Make up your mind, girl. What do you think?"

That's how it was that I went to work for Kelly Galligher. . . .

Barney's loud whoop suddenly brought my attention back to the table, the group around me. "Yes, yes, man. That's right," he cried. "Yes, that's exactly right."

I waited, knowing that soon somebody would explain to me what I had missed.

"It's the only sensible thing to do," James said in his measured way. "I wonder that we didn't think of it before. Don't you agree, Mary Ellen?"

I felt a blush rise in my cheeks. I stammered, "I. . . well, I . . . I'm sorry. I was woolgathering. I'm afraid I didn't hear just what . . ."

"We've decided," Sally said. "You will agree, won't you? You do see that it's the only way, don't you?"

"We'll keep the house," Barney said. "We'll live in it ourselves. We can rebuild it." His voice dropped. His cold blue eyes touched each of us in turn. "Yes, we can rebuild the house," he repeated, "and at the same time, we can rebuild ourselves."

4

IT was because I was remembering Kelly that I never knew who actually first made the suggestion.

Later on I tried to recreate the scene. I tried to play it back in my mind, to listen to what the various voices had said. But I was never able to make it come clear. There was only a confused background to my thoughts, and then, suddenly, James was asking, "Don't you agree, Mary Ellen?" and I had to confess that I hadn't been listening.

"We're rebuilding the house. Whatever needs doing, that is. And we'll rebuild ourselves at the same time," Barney said, repeating himself for my benefit.

"And we'll live rent free," Timothy put in. "That's a big thing. We'll have our checks to take care of our expenses, and share the costs for food. But we'll be living rent free."

"I don't know," Anne objected. She gave each of us a measured green glance full of suspicion. "How do we know that we'll get along?"

"Why shouldn't we?" James asked. "I feel I could get along very nicely with you."

She smiled faintly, acknowledging the compliment implied, but said in a dry tone, "We're not exactly old buddies. We don't know anything about each other."

"Who needs to know anything?" Sally cried. "I don't care. We're all cousins. That's what counts. And it's the only way we can make use of the house. And it would be crazy, just plain criminal, to let it go to waste."

"It does seem that way to me," Hester agreed. "And if it doesn't work out, well, then, nothing is lost. We can always just give it up, can't we?"

They were all watching me now, waiting, wondering what I would say, I knew.

I hesitated. It was easy enough for dimpled Sally to claim now that she didn't need to know anything about the rest of us.

But what if she had heard Carlotta's

hysterical accusations the night that Kelly died?

I shivered, the memory spilling cold into my blood, just as Carlotta's voice had spilled cold into my blood that awful night.

"You don't have anybody to hold you back, do you?" Barney was asking. "I'm talking about . . . well, you know, a boyfriend. Some man you don't want to leave, maybe. There isn't any reason, is there?"

I shook my head. My hair slid down over my cheek and I brushed it back impatiently. I had no one to leave. . . . There was no reason. . . . But then I thought of Mrs. George. I jumped to my feet, rocking the blue-checked table.

Barney grabbed my wrist, his fingers tight as steel. "Hey, where are you going?"

"I have to make a phone call. I forgot all about it. But . . ."

"A phone call? You? To whom? What about?" Barney's voice was suddenly hard, all laughter gone from him. His blue eyes were cold with suspicion.

I stammered, "The . . . the lady I live

56

with. She'll be wondering . . . I told her I'd . . ."

He drew my wrist to his lips, pressed a kiss on it. His beard tingled on my skin as he let me go, grinning apologetically. "Excuse me, Mary Ellen. I just thought you had figured out some way to do us out of the house, and were setting out to make your plans."

I stared at him. "It never occurred to me. Why would I do such a thing?"

"It could happen," he said silkily. "Go on, call the old lady, and then hurry back."

I phoned Mrs. George. I told her about Gentry Carrier, and the inheritance. I told her about the six others, my new-found cousins.

She twittered with excitement and pleasure. Somehow I couldn't mention the house to her, mention the decision we were making about it. That, I thought, I'd better explain face to face. It would be hard on her if I moved out. Not because of the money. She could easily rent the room, and I would make sure she had. But she had grown to like and depend on me, just as much as I liked and depended on her. I would miss her. But it seemed to me that if I were to have my share of the house then I would have to go there, live with the others. Thus, without consciously deciding, I found that I had already decided.

When I went back to the table, the others were laughing over fresh drinks. I knew they had reached an agreement without waiting for me.

But Barney asked softly, "Well, quiet Mary Ellen, what do you think?"

I drew a slow, careful breath. I hoped it would be all right. I must make it all right. "I guess I'll go along with the rest of you," I told him.

"I'm glad for you," Mrs. George said, her filmy eyes shining with tears. "You mustn't think that I'm not glad for you, Mary Ellen."

"I know," I said gently.

"It's just that I hate for you to go. In these few months we've been so close. It doesn't happen often. For people to get so close. I'm going to miss you something awful, Mary Ellen."

"I'll miss you, too, Mrs. George. But

I'll write to you every week. I promise. And as soon as I can, I'll come down and see you."

She twisted her red apron. From behind her, on the stove, the kettle whistled, but she ignored it. "It's so far away. Way up in the mountains. A terrible place. Point Janeway. It'll be cold, very cold. With winter coming on. And I never even heard of a town called Stony Ridge."

"It's just a wide place in the road, I guess. Mr. Carrier said there was a store and a gasoline station and not much else. But I'll bet buses go there, and so do the mails. So we'll be in touch."

"If there were just some other way," she said. "If only you could stay here with me. . . ."

"I couldn't think of anything," I admitted. "I did try, Mrs. George. And it was six to one, you see. We share and share alike. I couldn't very well go against the others, could I?"

"I understand that," she quavered, pursing her wrinkled lips, "but I don't like the sound of it. They're strangers. All strangers. What do you know of them?"

I smiled at her. "Now, Mrs. George . . . what do *they* know about me?"

"You?" she cried indignantly. "You? Why, anybody can look at you and know all they need to know. But strangers. . . ."

I grinned at her. "I think you're prejudiced in my favor. And besides, all these people are cousins of mine in some way. Very distant, that's true. But still, they *are* relations."

She brightened instantly. "Yes, of course. That's right. I was forgetting again, wasn't I? They *are* relations. That makes all the difference." She considered. Then, "Now tell me, just how does it come about?"

"I don't really know. The lawyer didn't explain."

"Just like a man," she said. "They never understand such things. It takes a woman to know whose great uncle was whose younger brother. But just as long as they're cousins. . . ."

I was glad that I had found the right words to give her peace of mind. Yet I wasn't sure that Gentry Carrier's vagueness had to do with a masculine inability to understand family lineage. I couldn't imagine a lawyer having that problem. I supposed he simply hadn't wanted to bother to take the time to explain.

I decided that when I saw him the next day I would make sure to get more information from him.

Meanwhile I would be getting ready to make the move that the seven of us had agreed on.

"I'm going to be sure that you have a roomer, you know," I told Mrs. George. "I won't leave until you have someone. So you won't be alone. And you'll have the rent coming in without any interruption."

She gave me a faint smile. "You're a dear child, Mary Ellen. You mustn't worry about that part of it. It's just that I hate to see you go. But it's something we must all bear. Love. And then partings. It's life. It's the good Lord's way."

At the end of that same week, I climbed into Barney's Volkswagen bus. It was crammed with suitcases and boxes, and people.

I had been surprised when Barney said he would drive us up to Point Janeway together, remembering that he told Gentry Carrier he had no car, no driver's license.

Barney had seen my brows rise, and grinned. "The old guy doesn't have to know everything, does he?"

"But why would you . . ."

"I lie to keep in practice," Barney laughed. And then, sobering, "No, quiet Mary Ellen . . . I just bought the bus for the trip, and got the license yesterday. You've got nothing to worry about."

I remember that, when I turned to wave goodbye to Mrs. George. She was standing on the cottage porch, her thin arm raised.

I had helped her prepare for the young college student who had rented my room. I had promised her that I would write. Now, with a sudden lump in my throat, I huddled in my seat, my shoulder pressing against Hester.

"Who's the old duck?" she asked.

"The lady I've been living with," I told her. "Mrs. George. She's very sweet."

"But she looks about ready to fall down and die," Hester said. "Old people are so. . . ." She shivered delicately, and I knew that she had suddenly realized that she, too, would age. Her red hair would fade to white and thin, and her smooth creamy skin would wrinkle, and her deep brown eyes would pale. "I don't like old people," she said. "They give me the willies."

I knew it was because she was afraid of what they reminded her of. But I wondered why she felt that way.

Anne said, "That Gentry Carrier. I hope he knows what he's doing. Wouldn't it be awful if we drove all that way up into the mountains, and there wasn't a Stony Ridge, or a Point Janeway?"

"You don't come on like a nervous chick," Barney laughed. "But you are. You really are. There's a house called Point Janeway, and there's a Stony Ridge."

"And just how do you know that?" she demanded.

"I checked a map for the town and the point. That's how I know," he retorted. He went on, "And I have a key to the house in my pocket."

"You do? Where did you get it?" Sally demanded. "I didn't know you had one. Did Gentry give it to you?"

"He did," Barney answered smugly.

"When we went in to tell him what we'd decided. He slipped it to me while you were all congratulating each other on your good sense."

"But how come?" Timothy asked. "Why didn't he tell the rest of us?"

"There's only one key, and only one bus. And I'm handling both of them," Barney answered.

Sally giggled. "Listen to the big shot." Then, "You are very much mistaken, Barney Gray, if you think that you're going to be running our lives. Just because we'll be living together doesn't give you any rights."

"I quite agree," James said. "It's something that ought to be well understood before we start out on our venture."

Barney just laughed. "Relax and enjoy it. Nobody is bossing anybody. We're all in this together. Equals. Together. Get it?"

I was thinking of that last meeting with Gentry Carrier. He had had a flushed and a hurried look. His breath was pure Bourbon and his eyes were more bloodshot than ever. He had stood in the waiting room, impatiently looking from one to another of us. "You are agreed? That's right? You'll keep the house, share it and live in it?"

Each of us nodded in turn.

"So be it," he said. "That just about ends my responsibility. I'll have the title drawn that way, and deposit it with the bank that handles the estate. Now, when will you move in?"

"As soon as possible," Barney said. "A couple of days. No more than that."

"It will take longer than that for the papers to be filed. You can examine them at the bank if you wish."

"When do your people mail out the checks?" Sally asked hopefully.

"The first of the month."

"Two weeks away," she breathed. "Oh, I can hardly wait."

Gentry didn't reply. He disappeared into the inner office for a moment. When he returned he was carrying a sheaf of papers. "All right then. If you'll sign at the bottom, our business will be concluded."

He passed a sheet to each of us. When he handed me mine, I said, "Mr. Carrier,

I'd like to know more about Ralph Dartmoor."

"There's nothing to know. Nothing that I can tell you. It goes so far back, you see. He has been dead more than four years. I am not prepared . . ."

Barney stepped between us. "Here you are, Mr. Carrier. The old John Hancock. Man, I tell you, I'm glad that's over and done. I never believed it. Not really. Not until this minute. Now that it's signed and sealed and delivered, I feel better. I can let myself go. I can breathe again."

"Not me," Sally said. "Not until I see that first check and know I can start saving for San Juan. Not until I see the house and know it's really there."

Gentry said, "And now, friends, I am on a tight schedule, so if you will excuse me."

There was no opportunity to question him further.

He and Barney swept us out of the office, and down the elevator, and into the street.

With a quick goodbye, Mr. Carrier climbed into a black Rolls Royce, and disappeared around the corner.

That was the last I had seen of him, though I had tried repeatedly to reach him by phone for the next two days. He hadn't been to his office, however, and he didn't have an answering service, I gathered, because no one replied, no matter how many times I called, not at any hour of the day or night.

"We're on our way," Barney said, his blue eyes gleaming. "We're leaving it all behind us here, and getting it all together there."

"I just want to see the house," Sally said. "That's all. I want to see the house. And then the check."

I knew just how she felt.

It was much the same for me. I still didn't believe in the inheritance. I didn't believe that something could happen so suddenly, so unexpectedly, so unexplainably. I didn't believe that life brought such desirable changes.

All through the long miles, I looked out the window at the autumn countryside, and tried to imagine what it would be like. I tried to picture Ralph Dartmoor, the man who had left all that he owned to a group of people related so distantly, and unknown to him. I tried to see the seven of us, living together, forming a new family.

But I suddenly found myself wishing that I hadn't left Mrs. George and her cottage. It had become home to me. I belonged there.

What lay ahead was undecipherable, the future written in a code I couldn't read.

What had been gold and glowing autumn in the lowlands was cold and gray in the mountains.

We left the fiery trees behind, the trailing scarlet vines, and moved into a place of mist hanging over bare black limbs, and damp granite piled in awkward monuments to unknown memories.

We arrived in Stony Ridge on the edge of a misty twilight.

Barney whistled softly as he pulled in to the side of the highway. "Carrier wasn't kidding about it's being a dead town."

I saw a gasoline station, obviously closed, because its pumps had been removed.

I saw a big brown toad of a house, its lit window covered with a home-made sign that identified it as a general store.

There was nothing else.

I was closest to the door so I was delegated to pick up a few provisions. Just what we would need for that night and the next morning.

Hester climbed out to help me.

We entered the store hesitantly. It was dim, empty.

The walls were lined with barren shelves and barrels. A few dusty cans stood on the floor. A jumble of penny candy filled a counter. A greasy looking meat box stood in a corner.

This was, I was sure, where the house's living room had once been. A curtained doorway seemed to lead to more rooms in the back.

Hester said, "Lovely place. I hope there's a supermarket some place close."

"I doubt it," I answered. Then, "And it doesn't look as if anybody's here either."

"We'll just see," Hester told me. She went back to the door, stamping her high-heeled shoes on the splintery boards. She opened the door, then hurled it shut with all her strength.

It snapped hard and fast. The sound it

made was like an explosion, and two cans tumbled down, making even more noise.

I winced, but Hester, in a satisfied voice, said, "That should do it all right."

We waited.

Within moments we heard slow shuffling footsteps. A voice called out, "Who is it? What do you want? I'm closed up. You know I'm closed up now so what do you want?"

"Some service. We need to buy some things," I said, adding hopefully, "If you don't mind."

An elderly man thrust the curtain aside, peered from the now exposed doorway. He had shaggy gray hair, and a long scooped nose. Tiny glasses hung on it as if about to slip off.

From behind him, peering out, too, were a small woman, and a tall, rail-thin bald headed man.

"I'm sorry to bother you," I said quickly. "But we do need some food. So if you wouldn't mind. . . ."

"All right. All right. Always in a hurry, you young people. Rush, rush, rush. Can't take a minute to breathe. Where do you think you're going in such a rush? Where

70

do you think it'll get you, I'd like to know."

He plainly didn't expect an answer. He went behind the counter, leaned on it. "Well? Well? What do you want? Just take it. Help yourself. Look around and find it and bring it here."

Hester grinned at me, and shrugged. She began to browse among the cans. She came back with pork and beans, and spinach and coffee. Meanwhile I had found eggs and bread. We loaded our purchases on the counter.

"Stocking up, are you?" he asked, looking down his nose and over his glasses. "Traveling through and stocking up. Well, every man to his own, I say. That's what I say."

"But we're not traveling through," I told him.

"Staying?" he echoed, his voice thin with disbelief. "Staying? Here in Stony Ridge? Nobody stays in Stony Ridge. I ought to know. I was born here, lived here all my life. My name is Josh Renner. The lady back there, she's my wife, Martha. The long drink of water is the postmaster, Asa Whalen. And that's his post office."

71

A wrinkled hand pointed to a table in the corner. "Open nine to five," Josh cackled. "Except Saturday. Then it's nine to twelve."

I smiled at Martha, at Asa. They stared back at me expressionlessly.

Josh went on, "So I know about Stony Ridge all right. It was a town once. It's not any more. It's not anything now. Everything torn down, blown down. Nothing left but this place. Nobody left but us three. You can ask me anything you want and I'll tell you. But mostly I'll tell you that nobody stays in Stony Ridge."

I introduced Hester and myself, then said, "We're going to be living in the Dartmoor house, at Point Janeway. Did you know him? Were you friends?"

Josh stared first at me, then at Hester. "You're going to be living there?" he cackled. "You two?"

"There are five more of us," Hester said coldly. "We're all cousins. He left the house to us, you see."

"He left it to you? Ralph did?"

Josh was looking at me, so I nodded.

"Ralph Dartmoor you say. That right?"

"Yes," I said. "That's right. Ralph Dartmoor."

"And you, you and the rest of you, you're figuring on staying out there? At Point Janeway?"

My heart began to beat very quickly.

Josh Renner's incredulity was frightening.

It meant something. But I didn't know what.

"Well? Well, is that it?" he demanded.

Behind him I saw Martha and Asa exchange meaningful glances.

I said as steadily as I could, "That's just what we plan to do. We're going to fix up the house and live there."

"You do whatever you want," Josh told me. "You'll do it no matter what. I know you young people. That's how you are. You'll do just what you want. But I'll say one thing, and just one thing. That Ralph . . . that Ralph Dartmoor, he didn't do you any favor."

5

RALPH DARTMOOR *didn't do you any favor. . . .*
I was so startled that I couldn't reply.

But Hester tossed her red hair, grinned. "That's a matter of opinion, isn't it?"

He looked her up and down over the top of his glasses. Then he transferred his gaze to me and did the same.

It was plain that he viewed neither of us with approval. It was so plain that I wondered if her fashionable green pants suit and my unfashionable skirt and sweater were not acceptable outfits in Stony Ridge.

At last he said, "It's a matter of fact. Not of opinion." And then, "This what you want?"

I nodded.

He made a row of figures on an old dirty brown bag. He added them quickly, the pencil skipping down the columns in his gnarled fingers. When he had a total, he thrust it at me. "Want to check?"

I took bills from my purse, smiled, "Oh, I'm sure it's right."

His stony eyes seemed to soften. "You're sure, huh? More fool you."

But he accepted the bills, packaged the items we had bought, and gave me my change.

"You don't have a whole lot here," Hester said.

"I got enough."

"But if there's nobody around, nobody except you, then how do you stay in business?"

"We don't need much," he cackled, "and what we need we got."

She persisted, "But who are your customers?"

"City people ought to stay in the city where they belong," he retorted. "That's what mountain people do. There's houses in all the canyons. There's people to do their shopping here. Summers we get travelers. We manage."

She shook her head, her brown gaze shifting from empty shelf to dusty counter. "Is there a supermarket around?"

I wished she had more tact. Josh Renner, his wife, and Asa Whalen, would be our closest neighbors.

But he grinned suddenly, revealing crooked yellow teeth. "County seat. It's a forty-mile drive. The hospital is there, and the police, and the supermarket, too. You can do it any time you want to."

I thanked him quickly, took the package from the counter. But then my curiosity about Ralph Dartmoor got the better of my judgment. I asked, "Mr. Renner, I'd like to get to know the people who knew Mr. Dartmoor, his friends."

"He didn't have any," Josh told me.

"He didn't? Why not?"

Josh shrugged.

Hester said, "Come on, Mary Ellen. What do you care about Ralph Dartmoor for? He's dead and gone and has been for four years."

"Right," Josh agreed.

I thanked him again, smiled at Martha and Asa, and received impassive stares in return.

I opened the door to leave.

Josh called, "You be careful, Mary Ellen. That road up to Point Janeway . . .

it's broken and curved and washed out in spots. And the house . . . well, it's pretty broken up, too. So mind how you go, as you go."

"We'll watch out," I promised.

"Lovely people, aren't they?" Hester said, as we went to the bus. "Warm. Hospitable. Friendly. Well, I tell you . . ."

"I guess they don't much care for strangers in Stony Ridge. A lot of small towns are like that."

Barney was waiting impatiently. "It took you a long time," he grumbled.

"That man in there is old, and slow-moving, and unfriendly," Hester retorted. "And you ought to see his wife. As well as the postmaster of Stony Ridge."

I settled myself in the Volkswagen, and repeated Josh Renner's warning about the road to Point Janeway for Barney's benefit.

He laughed, "There's no road I can't drive. And that's a fact."

Hester laughingly reported the rest of Josh Renner's remarks, and his answer to my questions about Ralph Dartmoor.

Barney shook his head. "Just what you'd expect."

"But it's odd," James said. "He must have, Ralph, I mean, been a hermit, wouldn't you say?"

"Maybe," Anne agreed. "But it doesn't matter to us."

"That's just what I was saying," Hester put in. "He's dead. So what's the difference."

I disagreed, but silently. Ralph Dartmoor did matter. It was he who had left us our small incomes, he who had brought us together to live in Point Janeway. I forebore to mention that to the others. If he didn't matter to them, so be it. Ralph Dartmoor, the man he had been, definitely mattered to me.

Barney's boast that there was no road he couldn't drive was soon proven true. He bounced the bus around sharply-angled curves and through washouts and from rut to rut as if he had made the same trip a dozen times before.

It seemed a long way, yet we had gone only half a mile or so from Renner's store, when the road suddenly ended before two stone pillars.

They appeared in our headlights like stationary and solid ghosts, and beyond them, at the rim of a long rocky slope, the house seemed to float in gray mist.

Barney grunted with satisfaction, arrowed between the pillars and jerked to a stop.

We all tumbled out, silent and staring.

I remembered again what Josh Renner had told me. *Ralph didn't do you any favor*.

Point Janeway was big, a low sprawling two-story place, its blistered walls broken irregularly by long narrow windows.

The whole of its first floor face was shadowed by a deep wooden porch. Six steps led up to it from the rocky slope. The whole of the area was covered with stunted, wind-gnarled black trees.

James said with a sigh, "It would seem that we have our work cut out for us."

I saw the broken wood of the steps, the sagging porch roof, and knew that he was right.

Anne muttered, "I can hardly wait to see what's inside." But her voice sounded doubtful.

A wind suddenly came up. It smelled of smoke, and rotting vegetation, and country.

I promised myself that I'd explore the area by day and sunlight, shivering in the misty dampness.

Barney climbed the slope, the rest of us trailing him. He unlocked the door, and threw it open. We followed him inside.

"Now," he said, "if everything worked out. . . ." He found a light switch, and a dusty chandelier spilled pale beams on us. "It did," he laughed. "Lights, gas, phone . . . we're all set up."

Sally tipped her blonde head, eyes aglow. "Oh, it's beautiful crystal. Just wait until I get it washed!"

"Anyhow, we'll have a roof over our heads," Timothy answered. "It may have holes in it for all we know. But it's a roof."

Barney turned through a wide arch, flicked another switch. A group of lamps came on, revealing a long dark living room, with a huge brick fireplace.

"Man," he said, loading the grate with a log that had been standing nearby, "this is going to be good. It's going to be home."

I heard his words with a strange reluctance. I thought of my small room at Mrs. George's cottage, the rose and lilac spread on my bed, the filmy white curtains at the window, the tiny kitchen in which we had had tea together.

I was suddenly sick with longing. That had been home. The only real home I had ever known.

But this, this vast sighing house set in the whispering trees was my home now. At least a seventh part of it was mine. Here someone related to me by blood had walked, and laughed. Here he had died. Surely some part of me belonged in this place.

Then why, I wondered, did I feel so much like an alien invader? Why did I feel so unwanted?

The big room was soon aglow with dancing flame and warmth. But it didn't touch the chill in my flesh. I told myself that I was over tired. I was allowing myself to be infected by the night, the wind, the shadows. I was reacting with the habit of insecurity, of fear and doubt, to what was new.

I went to look out of the windows that faced to the back of the house. I could see nothing but a vast misty emptiness.

Barney said, "That's where the rim slips

off into the valley." He stopped. Then, "At least I guess so. From the way Carrier described it to me. And down there some place there's the old quarry."

"Quarry?" Hester asked. "What's that?"

"Where they used to dig out stone, I imagine," James told her. "Or maybe still do."

"Not any more," Barney sighed. "Worse luck. If they did, we'd be making money off it. It's on our land."

Anne said, "Listen, I'm starving," and started us moving again.

We made short work of supper that night, picnicking in the dismal kitchen. Then we readied the bedrooms, and quickly retired, all of us tired by the journey and our labors; tired, perhaps, by our excitement, too.

Sally, sharing the room with me, murmured drowsily, "It's going to be okay, isn't it, Mary Ellen? We'll make it all right, won't we?"

"I guess so," I agreed cautiously.

"But we have to," she answered. "I gave up my job. Not that it was so much. But it was something. I don't have anything to fall back on now. And a job isn't all that easy to get."

I tried to reassure her, repressing my own doubts. "Like Timothy said, Sally. We have a roof over our heads. And the monthly checks, so . . ."

"I wish I'd gone to San Juan," she whispered. "I have the funniest feeling. I just know I should have gone to San Juan. I could have made a new start there. And that's what I should have done. Really made a new start."

She sighed deeply. Soon after, hearing her long slow breaths, I realized that she was asleep.

I lay awake, tense under my quilts. Why did Sally feel that she needed a new start? I wondered. What was it that she wanted so desperately to leave behind her?

Was there, in her past, something she wanted to forget?

Did she hope that here, now, with Ralph Dartmoor's help, she could move forward into a happier and more free future?

If that were so, we had another bond in common. I, too, hoped to forget painful memories. . . .

I had let Kelly Galligher talk me into being his companion, and moved to the mansion in which he lived with his daughter Carlotta, and her husband, Jim Henry.

She was in her early thirties. A thin, tall, intense dark-haired woman, nervously suspicious. Her husband was a state senator and was being spoken of as the possible next governor.

Kelly had his own wing, completely separate from the main part of the building, with Mark and Julie Gormley to care for him. In the six months I was there we formed a small self-contained family.

Carlotta crossed the terrace for occasional visits, eyeing me narrowly, questioning me about how I had met Kelly, and my background. Jim Henry came even less frequently.

Very soon after I joined him, Kelly said, "Mary Ellen, I want you to do me a favor. How about you call me Kelly instead of Mr. Galligher. Mr. Galligher . . . it's too formal, not friendly."

To please him, I tried it, expecting that the familiarity would embarrass me. Instead I found it peculiarly comfortable.

A strange closeness grew up between us very quickly. It was as if the barrier of age didn't exist. He talked to me about his earlier life.

"I was a man with appetites," he said once. "I couldn't understand the need to control them. Now I know. It takes age to teach some men. Years to make them see. What good is knowing too late, Mary Ellen?"

"Maybe it's supposed to be that way," I suggested.

"Maybe it is. But if I had known then, it would be different. Mary Ellen, do you believe me? Do you know I'm telling you the truth? I would never have allowed it to be as it is. If I had known then."

I nodded without really understanding, wanting only to soothe him.

"I keep thinking of Marianna. Poor woman. Was it her fault she went mad? Was it mine?"

He said nothing more then. Later, when I asked Julie, she frowned. "Marianna? Is he talking about her?" And then, "Best not to encourage it, Mary Ellen. It makes him sad. She was his wife. Carlotta's mother. She was in an institution for years before she died. If you ask me Carlotta's got the same blood in her, and the boy, Benjamin, has it, too."

"Benjamin? I never heard . . ."

"You won't either. Kelly never mentions him. Benjamin is a wild one. He's been gone away these five years, and good riddance to bad rubbish."

One night, an hour after dinner, Carlotta came in. She gave me a cold, narrow-eyed look, said, "Dad, I want to talk to you alone."

Kelly sighed, "What now?"

I quickly excused myself, glad to escape her oppressive presence, and settled down to read in the study down the hall. But her shrill angry voice penetrated the closed door. I couldn't quite hear the words, and I didn't like being an involuntary eavesdropper so I went to my room.

Soon after I heard the tap of footsteps on the flagstone terrace, and glanced out. Carlotta ran past the window and on to the main part of the house.

I waited, thinking that Kelly would ring for me. As it grew late, and I still didn't hear the bell, I became uneasy. I went down the quiet, shadow-filled hall to the living room.

The lamp was still burning.

Kelly was in his wheel chair, his head tipped to one side, his eyes wide open.

The pink pillow I had made for him as a head rest was on the floor on top of the velvet throw.

With a sudden shivering in my heart, I knew that he was dead.

Mark spoke to the Henrys immediately, then called the doctor. I waited with Kelly's body, my eyes stinging with held-back tears.

Carlotta came in like a whirlwind, screaming, "What did you do to him? He was all right when I left. He was fine, laughing, when I left him."

I remembered her shrill angry voice coming through the walls of the study, and how she had run across the terrace.

"What happened? What did you do?" she screamed. "It's your fault. Yours. He was going to send you away, wasn't he? So you. . . ."

I shrank beneath the attack, speechless and horrified. I couldn't answer her. I didn't know what had happened to Kelly.

The doctor said, "He was a very old man, Carlotta. He slept away. It's a mercy to have such an end. You must accept that and be grateful."

I looked at the pink pillow on the tangled velvet throw and wondered if I imagined the speculative stare in the doctor's eyes.

His words, his calm, seemed to quiet Carlotta. She allowed herself to be put to bed, eased by sedation.

She never spoke to me again. I never even knew if she remembered her hysterical words.

After Kelly's funeral Jim Henry said, "Mary Ellen, I hope you've forgiven Carlotta, and forgotten her behavior when her father died. It was shock, you know."

I nodded, not answering. I hadn't forgotten it, but there seemed nothing to say. I knew I could never forget her terrible words. Why had they been in her mind? I knew she had always disliked me, but how had I offended her?

Jim said smoothly, "You'll be looking for another job. I want to make it easier. Kelly was fond of you. I shall give you a half year's salary as a bonus. You could move to another town. The bonus will make it possible."

"You don't owe me anything," I said.

"Of course not. But Kelly would have wanted it. And then, Carlotta's behavior deserves an apology. I feel a nest egg can help."

It would have helped, but I didn't want to profit by Kelly's death. I told Jim, "I don't want a bonus. I'm not moving away."

"If you should change your mind, have trouble getting a job. . . ."

"I'll manage," I told him, not knowing what was ahead of me.

That day I found the room in Mrs. George's cottage. Mark and Julie helped me move my things. They promised they would keep in touch. A month later I received a post card from them. The Henrys had gotten them a job with some people in Florida. I never heard from them again.

I found it harder to get work than I ever had before. Each lead I went on faded. I was desperate, fearful, when I heard from Gentry Carrier. . . .

Sally thrashed in her bed suddenly, moaned.

I sat up, peered at her.

"Oh, no," she moaned. "Oh, no. I'll never do it again. No, I couldn't ever go back. I swear I'll never have to go back."

I whispered, "Sally, wake up. You're having a nightmare."

She went silent, gasping. After a moment, she rolled over to face me. "What's the matter?"

"I think you were having a bad dream. Don't you remember?"

"But how do you know?" she demanded.

"You groaned, said something."

"You mean I was talking?" Her voice was suddenly shrill. "What did I say, Mary Ellen? What did I say?"

I knew what she had said, but I could see barely-controlled fear well up in her. I said casually, "Oh, Sally, how do I know what you said? Some gibberish. Nothing that made sense."

She sank back, yawned. "Oh, I was wondering what on earth I could have talked about." She rolled over, breathed slowly, pretending to go back to sleep.

But I knew that she must be thinking about her dream, wondering what I had understood of her words.

I knew that she was afraid.

6

I AWAKENED early.

The house was still. Wisps of fog hung at the window like the white curtains in Mrs. George's cottage.

I dressed quickly in jeans and sweater, wondering if the sun ever shone on Point Janeway.

When I started down, I discovered that there were two flights of stairs. One was at the back of the hall, and entered the kitchen, while the other was at the front and opened into the lower foyer.

I finally found my way into the kitchen.

Hester was standing over the coffee pot, urging it to start perking. "This place looks even worse by dawn's early light," she grinned.

"We have our work cut out for us," I agreed.

When the coffee was ready, we had two cups each, and decided to go exploring.

We went out the kitchen door past a

stack of firewood, then picked our way down the rocky slope.

The fog had lifted by then, but scarves of mist still hung in the bare trees.

Hester skidded on a rock, and stumbled to her knees. A gold chain flashed at her throat, weighted by two narrow rings.

She straightened, saw me looking at them. She flipped the ring-bearing chain under her sweater, grinning at me. "That's right," she said. "Wedding rings. Two of them. And don't ask me why I keep them. For souvenirs maybe. Or reminders."

"I didn't realize you'd been married."

"Twice. Two dumb mistakes." She walked on, and I followed her.

The small stunted black trees became sparse.

The rocky path led down until it suddenly ended at the edge of a deep pit.

It had smooth steep white walls, and far below, it was filled with dark green water.

Hester moved back, her brown eyes flickering. "The quarry." She wrapped her arms around herself in a hug. "I don't like this, Mary Ellen."

"It looks deep," I said.

She took another step back, and turned.

93

"Let's go up to the house. The rest of them should be stirring by now."

The next few weeks passed quickly.

The seven of us were busy setting the house to rights. We were frightened by our first study of the place by daylight. It wasn't just the broken front porch steps, and its sagging roof, we had found. Point Janeway was a shambles inside and out. It seemed to have been vacant for more than four years.

"It blows your mind, what can happen with time," Barney had said.

"I begin to see now why the house is unsalable," James had agreed.

"But when we get finished," Barney chuckled, "the situation will be different."

I, listening, wondered. We'd find no buyer in Stony Ridge. Then where would one come from?

"What's the use of thinking about selling?" Anne asked. "We haven't really moved in yet."

We agreed, after much discussion, to go about the work systematically. We listed the repairs that had to be done, moving from room to room.

"That fireplace . . . take a look at the loose bricks," Barney said. "They've got to be mortared in, or the house will go up in flames."

"Broken windows," Timothy called out. And then, sighing, "The family's house had French windows, floor to ceiling, and exposed beams."

Hester banged her foot expressively, and a step crackled and splintered. That went on the list, too.

It was long by the time we were finished. But, surprisingly, what had seemed, at the start, an insurmountable task, proved easier than we had thought.

I was able to buy most of what Barney and the other men needed at Josh Renner's place, and what he didn't have himself he somehow located for us.

Barney was astonishingly capable.

I told him so one morning. I was on the porch, handing him nails, and watching as he hammered new boards into the steps.

He slanted a cold blue look at me. "Yes," he said. "I know how to do things. I've been on my own, making it however I could, for a long time. That's how you learn."

"I guess maybe it is."

"Quiet Mary Ellen. You look at my long hair and my gold earring and you wonder. But you're much too polite to ask."

I had wondered about him. His dress, his speech. . . .

He said quietly, "I might as well tell you. I know you won't turn me in. Why should you?" And went on, "I've been on the run, you see. If I can hold out one more year, then maybe I'll be home free."

"On the run?" I echoed.

"The draft," he said briefly. "I don't plan on getting sucked into the army, thanks a lot."

I sat back on my heels, shocked and a little queasy.

"You don't have to like it," he grinned. "It's got nothing to do with you."

"I'm not your judge, Barney," I answered. "It's your conscience you have to deal with."

He took a nail from my limp fingers, banged it into the board. "Be a good chick, Mary Ellen. Keep the bad news to yourself."

I promised him that I would, and we

never spoke about it again, but, of course, I never forgot it.

The repair work went smoothly enough, and as it was finished, the girls and I systematically cleaned the house from top to bottom. When that was done we tackled the old shed, clearing out broken tools, and cans of dried paint, until Barney shooed us away, saying it was man's work and we'd get our fingers caught in a bear trap if we weren't careful.

Gradually over those two weeks, we got to know one another, but it was a surface knowing. It didn't seem to matter then. It was only later that I began to see a pattern.

I made most of the trips in to Stony Ridge to pick up supplies.

Timothy drove me in the Volkswagen bus, and came in to Renner's only when I needed help in carrying out the supplies I got.

Perhaps that was why the others didn't take seriously what I told them about the Renners and Asa Whalen, and how they felt about us.

Josh was always polite to me, his courtesy masking a hostility that was quite open in the other two.

Martha always watched me as if she expected me to steal something if she turned her gray eyes away for a moment.

Asa always grumbled, "Here's the stuff," and slapped the few circulars we received, and my occasional letter from Mrs. George on the table, ignoring my hopeful attempts at conversation.

I didn't know what was wrong with him, with Martha. I couldn't see why Josh had taken a dislike to me. I had always gotten along well with people of their generation. I was obscurely troubled by their open disapproval.

I mentioned it to Timothy one day.

He shook his bald head, grinned, "You're an innocent, Mary Ellen."

"What do you mean?"

"Why, they're old, and don't understand. They've got the idea that we're . . . we're. . . ." His round face turned pink. He looked away from me. "They think we're shacking up together, as Barney would say."

It was something that hadn't occurred to me. I said, "But I told them we're cousins."

"So what? Who says they have to

believe you? And who says it's true anyway?"

Oddly, it was that, Timothy asking, "Who says it's true anyway?" that stirred my uneasiness, forgotten in the adventure of getting settled in Point Janeway.

I began to think about it again, and the more I did, the more I wondered. I didn't see how we could be cousins, even distant ones. I didn't see how Gentry Carrier had managed to locate us, each one, except for Barney, living in the same city, but unknown to each other.

I could see no way at all in which I might deserve a portion of Ralph Dartmoor's estate.

I told Sally about my doubts as we were preparing to go to bed one night, saying, "I wish Gentry Carrier had explained a llttle more clearly. But somehow every time I asked him he seemed to brush me off."

Sally grinned, "Maybe you shouldn't ask so many questions."

"I wish I knew though."

"Don't. Beggars can't be choosers, can they? And looking gift horses in the mouth can be a terrible mistake."

"But just the same. . . ."

"Listen, nobody's come and thrown us out. The first set of checks arrived just when the lawyer said they would. We're all satisfied. We're getting along. Why don't you just forget it?"

I tried to, but I couldn't. The vague uneasiness grew stronger. I began to feel like an impostor, enjoying a life that by rights should not have been mine.

I decided one morning to call Gentry Carrier.

I couldn't get through. I was told there was no such listing at the address I gave. I repeated the name, the address carefully. "He's an attorney," I insisted. "He must have a phone."

The operator told me to hold on. Within moments, she told me the listing had been discontinued. No change had been entered. I asked her to check under lawyers. She soon told me that no lawyer of that name was recorded.

Puzzled, I put down the phone. I couldn't figure out what that meant. Where had Gentry Carrier gone? Why had he given up his phone? Did that mean he had given up his office, too?

I turned to find James in the doorway. His thin face was tense. "What are you trying to call him for?"

"I wanted to ask him something."

"What something?"

"I thought he might have more information . . . about my family, I mean."

James' shoulders slumped. His fingers played with his tie. "What's the sense of it? What do you care?"

I didn't answer him.

Later he told the others.

Barney said, "Carrier doesn't know anything. You're just rocking the boat."

"You must be up to something," Anne said suspiciously. "Don't try any funny business, Mary Ellen."

I didn't answer her either.

I kept wondering what had happened to Gentry Carrier. It seemed odd that he should have disappeared. Then I realized that I might be jumping to conclusions. For all I knew, he had gone on vacation and disconnected his phone temporarily.

I began to wonder how I could check that. I didn't want to ask Mrs. George to make a trip to his office, to see if it was still there. It would be hard on her, and it might raise troubling questions in her mind. I decided that some way or other I must find a pretext for returning to the city. Explaining to the others would only evoke more disapproval.

Asa Whalen handed me a letter from Mrs. George when I picked up the mail. I made that the excuse, and when I got back to Point Janeway I announced that the next morning I would take the daily bus to the city to visit her, and return the following afternoon.

Anne narrowed her green eyes at me. "Are you running away already, Mary Ellen?"

I smiled at her, but I wondered why that should have occurred to her. I said, "I'll be back when I told you."

Speculation was in her voice, answering, "You've got a bee in your bonnet." It was in her slow smile as she went on, "You can't be homesick for the old gal after just barely more than two weeks."

"Maybe I am," I confessed, thinking of the small wren-thin woman, her quiet cottage, the room in which I had felt so at home. "Maybe that's just what it is."

I considered that might be the real

source of my uneasiness. Perhaps the whole trouble lay in the feeling of isolation I had.

The others seemed to have accepted their good fortune as due them, accepted it and settled down to be happy with it. Yet I found myself waiting for something, anxiously aware of a wrongness that I couldn't identify.

Timothy offered to drive me to Stony Ridge, but I decided to walk. I made the bus in plenty of time. As I boarded it in front of Renner's, I saw Josh and Martha peering out at me.

Mrs. George greeted me with tears in her filmy eyes. "I didn't think you'd come back to see me," she said.

"But I promised I would."

"Do you like it there? Will it be all right?" she asked, hurriedly leading me to the kitchen, and setting about the preparation of tea.

"It's pleasant. We've fixed up the house." I stopped on the brink of describing it to her. I stopped because, quite suddenly, now that I was here in the familiar kitchen, I realized what I hadn't realized before.

We had repaired and cleaned and polished Point Janeway, and yet, somehow, the house remained what it had been before we went to work. There were no more broken floor boards or steps or windows. There was no dirt. Yet there was also no glow to the furniture, no sparkle to the windows, no brightness in the crystal chandelier that Sally had so carefully washed. The house resisted us because there was no love within its walls. Just as Mrs. George's cottage accepted her because there was.

Now she asked quickly, "What is it, Mary Ellen?"

I went on. I told her about Point Janeway, the two sets of stairs, the high narrow windows, the rocky slope that led to the quarry and the valley below. I told her about Sally and Anne and Hester, about Timothy and James and Barney.

She listened, nodding her gray head. Finally she said, "But will it be all right?"

"I think so."

"Then why are you doubtful?"

I didn't know how to explain my uneasiness. I didn't want to mention the trouble I'd had trying to reach Gentry Carrier.

Mrs. George went on quickly, "You can always come back, Mary Ellen. If you don't like it, forget your share of the house, and come back to me. Juney is a sweet girl, and she'll understand. She'd give up the room for you."

After we'd had our tea, I went to the lawyer's office.

The building looked even more run-down. There was another "For Rent" sign tacked to the entrance. I took the wheezy elevator to the third floor, and went down the corridor to the end. The glass door on which Gentry Carrier's name had been printed in gold was blank now, and hung open. I went inside. The room was empty, bare, dust streaked. The inner office was the same.

Gentry Carrier was gone as if he had never existed.

But I knew that he had. He had written a letter to me, and I had seen him with my own eyes when I had visited him in response to it. I'd seen him, caught the odor of bourbon on his breath, looked into his bloodshot eyes. And I'd received a check from the bank just as he had promised.

Surely the man existed. Then where had he gone?

I went downstairs to look for the building superintendent, but couldn't find him. I did find an occupied office on the first floor. When I opened the door, a small, red-faced man looked up in surprise from the newspaper he had been reading. I asked him about Gentry Carrier. The small man chewed on his cigar and shrugged. "They come and they go. I don't know anything about him."

"But when did he move?"

"Don't ask me. I haven't the faintest."

I asked who might know, and the small man shrugged again.

I saw that there was nothing to be gained here, and decided to go to the bank which had sent the check. I found its address in the phone book, and made my way there.

I was surprised by how difficult it was to get information. All I wanted to know was Gentry Carrier's new address. I reasoned that since it was he who had arranged the disposition of Ralph Dartmoor's estate the bank would know how to reach him.

A Mr. Olsen spoke to me. I explained what I wanted twice, and he shook his head twice.

"That's quite impossible, Miss Christian," he said. "We give out no information." He didn't give me a chance to explain a third time. He went on, "You have received the first check, haven't you?"

"Yes. That's not it. I just want to know . . ."

He cut in, "Miss Christian, the fund was desposited to our Trust Department. It is to be divided, a monthly check sent to those listed. That is all I can tell you, all I know."

I thanked him and left no wiser than when I had so hopefully arrived.

It was at the next corner that I saw the picture. It caught my eye as I passed the club entrance. I stopped because the girl looking out at me looked so much like Anne. She had the same long green eyes, the same sultry smile. She wore a filmy shawl and nothing else to conceal her curved body. The name under it was simply Anita. I stood still, staring at the familiar face. Was that Anne? The Anne I knew? Or was that someone else? A double for Anne who, as she had done, too, danced in a night club.

The door behind me whispered open.

I turned.

A dark cadaverous-looking man examined me from head to toe. "You looking for work?" he asked finally.

"No. I . . . I just thought this . . ." I pointed at the picture, "I thought I recognized a friend of mine."

"Did you, or didn't you?" he asked.

"Anne, not Anita, is her name."

The dark man grinned. "Anita . . . that's for the blue lights. Anne . . . that's for real. But she doesn't work here any more. And if she's smart she won't show her face on the street either. Tell her if you see her."

"But why? What do you mean?"

"The boss is still pretty sore at her. She tried to say she wasn't involved. But when one of the good customers starts yelling that he's been taken for a big roll, and names names, then she can deny it all she wants. But if he decides to give her one more chance when she begs for it, and she all of a sudden walks off, without a thank you or a by your leave, then the boss gets mad. And I mean mean mad."

"I don't think it possible . . ." I began. But I knew it was. She had said she wanted to get away from her night club job. Now I saw why.

"A con is a con," the cadaverous man shrugged, and let the door slam shut in my face.

The next afternoon as the bus wheels hummed on the wet highway, I wished I hadn't gone into the city.

I had only confirmed the lawyer's disappearance, and confirmed my uneasiness at the same time. I felt more than ever anxious to find information about my unknown family through Ralph Dartmoor.

I had learned that Anne was accused of some sort of confidence game.

It was still pouring when I arrived in Stony Ridge.

I called Point Janeway, and Timothy promised to pick me up. I waited in Renner's.

"You got one more out there," Josh told me. "It's going to be crowded if you keep taking them in."

"You mean there's a new person?"

"That's right."

"But who?" I asked, bewildered by the news. There had been only seven of us. Who could the eighth be?

"How do I know who?" Josh retorted. "I don't even know who the rest of you are, do I?"

Behind him, looking through the curtain, Martha snorted.

Asa grumbled over the envelopes on his table.

"I've told you about them," I protested, "and you know me, and. . . ."

Josh agreed. "Yes, you've told me," in a voice thick with disbelief.

I suddenly thought of Gentry Carrier again. While I had been in the city, could he have come up here to Point Janeway?

Soon Timothy pulled up before Renner's.

He leaned out, waved at me.

A man was sitting in the bus beside him.

But it wasn't Gentry Carrier. I knew that at a single glance.

It was someone I had never seen before.

7

THE stranger got out, waited while I hurriedly told the Renners and Asa Whalen goodbye, and hurried outside to the Volkswagen.

His hair was very dark and wavy, but cut short and smooth. He was tall, lean, with a hawk's arrogant grace of body, and the suggestion of a hawk's leashed-in strength. He wore blue trousers, a heavy blue sweater, a white collar showing at his strong throat.

Timothy said, "Mary Ellen, this is Glencarlyn. He's a friend of Anne's."

I tried not to remember what I had learned in the city. I was determined not to give Anne away.

Glencarlyn nodded at me, very blue eyes sweeping up and down in a quick glance. His narrow lips smiled faintly.

I acknowledged the introduction, and climbed into the bus.

He swung in after me.

Timothy drove out of the village

quickly, as if he were making an escape, I thought.

Glencarlyn was quiet.

I felt, rather than saw, the quick sizing-up glances he gave me.

The silence went on uncomfortably long. At last, to break it, I asked, "What's been happening, Timothy?"

"Point Janeway still stands. If that's what you want to know. It'll never be like my family's place. It just doesn't have the charm. But it's there. Did you think it maybe fell down since yesterday morning?"

I grinned, shook my head.

Yes, I'd only been gone over night, but it seemed much longer to me. I felt as if I had traveled a great distance, taken days for the journey.

The closer we came to Point Janeway, the greater my uneasiness. Gentry Carrier had disappeared. I didn't know why.

He had been the only link to the mysterious person who had left me and the others our inheritance, the bequest which had brought us together in Ralph Dartmoor's house.

I wondered if I should tell the others

about the lawyer's disappearance. But I was strangely unwilling to.

They would immediately begin to worry about the next month's check. They would blame me if something went wrong, and we were left high and dry with only the house and nothing on which to run it. And they would want to know why I had sought Gentry Carrier in the first place. How would I answer that question? I didn't think I would know how to put my vague suspicions into words. Perhaps they were nothing. Perhaps they represented a feeling of unworthiness on my part.

Glencarlyn asked suddedy, "Where did you go?"

I didn't quite know what he meant. I turned, gave him a questioning look. Our glances met and held. I saw something watchful in his blue eyes, something oddly at variance with his casual tone.

"You were away," he said finally. "I was just wondering."

"I went to see a friend of mine in the city."

He nodded.

Timothy nodded. "I guess you really did, too. What I thought was that you'd gone to shop. To spread around some of your new-found wealth."

"Not quite yet," I answered. "I have a feeling I'd just better wait and see how things go."

"Sensible girl," Timothy told me. "Now Sally, she's already spent her first check in her head three times, and I'll bet she'll be spending it in fact within days."

"Maybe not. She's still talking about going down to San Juan."

And then I remembered. Sally had wanted to go to San Juan, to make a new start. She had cried out in her sleep, "I won't go back. I can't," and been frightened when I awakened her, frightened that she might have revealed some secret in her sleep. Barney had slanted a cold blue look at me, and told me that he was a draft evader on the run. And just the day before, quite by accident, I had learned that Anne, calling herself Anita, had been accused of being part of some night club con game.

I shivered, watching the wind-driven rain lash the stunted black trees. Sally, Barney, Anne . . . each of them had turned their backs on the past when they came to Point Janeway.

The bus jolted over potholes, skidded through the washed-out spots on the road.

"We're going to have to fix this up one of these times," Timothy said.

"It would take a lot of money, wouldn't it?" I asked.

"Some. But if we all put in a little it wouldn't be so bad. And this is rough on the bus and our bones."

Glencarlyn laughed. "I thought I'd broken all my springs coming in. And I didn't even know where I was going."

"You mean you couldn't get directions to the house?" I asked.

"I mean I didn't even know there was a house."

I looked at him blankly, and saw a faint gleam of laughter in his eyes; the corners of his mouth twitched.

He went on, "I was just loafing along when I saw this road. I figured it went some place, so I took it."

But Timothy had said he was a friend of Anne's, I remembered. If he was, then did he expect me to believe that he had accidentally come upon her, here in this isolated spot?

He said, "I got some place all right. To the ridge, and then the quarry. I'm afraid I scared Anne halfway to death. She was sleeping on the rocks, and I very nearly tramped on her. By the time we got ourselves sorted out, the rains came. She took me up to the house with her to dry off. And I stayed over."

I noticed that he had clearly explained how he happened to know Anne, to be at Point Janeway. I wondered why he troubled to. It was none of my business. But somehow I was pleased to know the truth of it.

"It's a beautiful place," he went on.

"The house?" Timothy groaned.

Glencarlyn laughed. "I wasn't thinking of that. I meant the ridge, the quarry. . . ."

"Don't let our Hester hear you say that. She's developing a thing about it. It's the best view of the valley, but she says it spooks her."

"Why?" Glencarlyn asked.

Timothy shrugged. "Ask her."

"You've got an unusual arrangement,"

116

Glencarlyn said. "The seven of you. Living together."

"It works out," Timothy said.

It's worked out so far, I thought silently. But it's only been just over two weeks.

"Yes," Glencarlyn said. "Anne explained it to me." He gave me that faint smile again. "I have to admit I'm jealous. I like the idea of having a private hotel."

"It's something like that," Timothy said.

"And it's just what I want."

"A private hotel? What for?" Timothy asked.

"I'm a writer. I've just been driving around, looking for a new spot to settle in for a month or so. I don't want to stay in a hotel or motel. That's just too . . . well, it's too formal a thing, if you get what I mean. This . . . your place, your arrangement, would be perfect for me."

Timothy chuckled, "Then get yourself a bunch of cousins and talk them into buying some property."

"Getting a bunch of cousins isn't so easily arranged," Glencarlyn retorted.

But I thought that maybe it was. It

could be. If one knew how to do it. If one knew how to research families, probably any person could find all sorts of cousins he'd never known he had before. That was, wasn't it? exactly what had happened to me? Or was it? What did I know of the six with whom I had thrown in my lot? The question answered itself. I knew very little about them. No more, surely, than I knew about Glencarlyn, whom I had met only moments before.

Timothy braked the bus before the gray stone pillars, then skimmed between them, and stopped with a jolt on the slope.

"I feel good in this place. Whenever I get close to it, I get a right feeling. I could work here. I know it," Glencarlyn said.

"Then why don't you stay?" Timothy asked. "If there's one thing we've got a lot of it's beds."

I had the feeling that Glencarlyn had been working up to that suggestion. That Timothy, without realizing it, had been maneuvered into making it.

Glencarlyn looked thoughtful. "I could, maybe. If the others agreed."

Timothy nodded, got out of the bus, made a dash through the rain up the slope.

Glencarlyn opened the door, slid out, and waited for me to join him.

Cold drops stung my cheeks as I stumbled toward the porch.

He didn't seem to notice them. He said, "What do you think? Would I be imposing? I'd pay my share of food, of course, and something for rent, too."

"I don't know," I told him breathlessly, "see what the others say, why don't you?"

We got to the porch finally. He offered me his handkerchief and I wiped my face and hair.

Anne came out, smiling. "Hi," she said. "How was the trip?"

But she wasn't looking at me. Her bright, emerald-green eyes were fixed on Glencarlyn. Her slow exotic smile was for him. I knew that she wouldn't object to having Glencarlyn stay on as a paying guest.

Very soon I saw that the same held true for Hester and Sally.

When we gathered for dinner that evening, they were each of them, and for the first time since we had moved in together, very dressed up.

Anne wore a filmy black see-through

blouse, and tight black stretch pants, an outfit that reminded me of the picture I'd seen of her the day before.

Hester was in a brief green mini skirt.

Sally had on a white peasant blouse with a scooped neck, and a bright red skirt that swirled around her.

I was uncomfortably aware of my plain black pants, and my man's shirt with the sleeves rolled to the elbow. But in a way, I was glad that I hadn't taken special note of Glencarlyn's presence. With Sally and Anne and Hester so obviously vying for his attention, I felt well out of it. Let them fight over him for as long as he stayed, I thought.

Barney and Timothy didn't seem to notice or care.

But I slowly realized that James' not quite real English accent was heavier than ever, that his slate eyes went more and more often to Anne, that his hands plucked ever more frequently at his tie.

It didn't surprise me when Glencarlyn said, speaking to the group as a whole, "Timothy and Mary Ellen came up with a great idea on the way back from Stony Ridge. At least I think it was a great idea."

Barney tipped back his head. The long dark hair swung on his shoulder. His single gold loop earring sparkled. "I'm always open to great ideas. What's it about, man?"

"That I stay on here for a month or so. If the rest of you agree, of course."

"Stay on?" James asked, shooting a quick look at Anne.

"I told you I was looking for a place to light, and this seems good to me. I like the bunch of you, and the setting. I could work here, I know." Glencarlyn grinned, "And I wouldn't be a free loader. I'd pay room and board."

"That's what we could use for fixing up the road," Timothy put in.

"And besides, I think you could do with another pair of man's hands when you get to that," Glencarlyn went on. "I wouldn't mind putting my back into it to help."

Barney shrugged. "Why not? If you want to."

Anne's slow exotic smile flashed quick and hot. "Say, that's great."

Sally dimpled her agreement.

Hester said, "That gives us a better

balance, doesn't it? Four girls and four men."

A quick flush touched my cheeks. I wished she hadn't said that, but no one else seemed to notice, to mind.

"Then it's settled," Glencarlyn said. "I'm glad."

That was how, so easily and quickly, he inserted himself in our midst. That was how the seven became eight.

Sally was brushing her curly blonde hair. She gave it quick hard strokes, peering at herself in the mirror, watching her plump wrist turn and pull. "I should have gone with you, Mary Ellen," she was saying. "If I'd had any sense that's what I'd have done."

"You can ride down tomorrow. Or the next day," I told her. "What difference does it make?"

"Only I was due today . . . I mean, I have a lot of things I want to buy. And I shouldn't have put it off."

"I still don't see . . ."

"Not that it makes so much difference. It's just . . . I hate to make the trip alone."

"Maybe Anne or Hester want to shop, too," I suggested.

Sally grinned. "Bet? They won't leave. Not while Glencarlyn's here."

I laughed. "Oh, come on, Sally."

"And I don't blame them," she went on. "He's a doll. Haven't you noticed?"

I had noticed that he was attractive. I had been aware of the blueness of his eyes, the faint smile that touched his narrow lips. I certainly wouldn't admit that aloud.

But Sally didn't suffer from that kind of reticence. She said, "I hate to leave myself. He's . . . well, he's quite a man."

"Then forget your shopping for a while," I laughed. "You don't really have to buy . . ."

"I do," she said. "I'd better go in tomorrow."

She shivered as she spoke, and then tightened her lips.

It was the sound of muted weeping that awakened me.

I thought at first that I must be still asleep and dreaming. The room was dark, shadowed. I heard the wind moaning at the window and the whisper of rain, and then I heard again the muffled gasp for breath, the choked sob.

123

I spoke up. I asked softly, "Sally? Sally, what's the matter?"

"I can't," she said. "Oh, I can't go back. Not now. Not when everything's so different. I just couldn't . . . if I'd only known. . . ."

I slipped from my bed, bent over her. "Sally?"

Her wide-open eyes gleamed with tears. She shook her head from side to side. "Oh, Mary Ellen, what should I do? Tell me what I should do."

"But about what? What's wrong? What are you scared of?"

"I can't," she whispered. "Leave me alone. Just leave me alone, I tell you." She buried her face in her pillow, shoulders shaking with sobs I could no longer hear.

I waited for a moment, then I went back to bed. If she wouldn't share her trouble with me there was nothing I could do, but I made up my mind that I would find out what was wrong. I would help her if I could.

Her eyes were still somewhat swollen the next morning, but she pretended to me that there had been no midnight weeping, no anguished protests against some unspecified fear. She announced that she would be going into the city as soon as she finished helping with the breakfast dishes, and Timothy promised to drive her to Stony Ridge.

I went along for the ride, and to pick up the mail.

Sally disappeared on to the bus, waved as it pulled out and swung onto the highway.

Timothy waited for me while I went into Renner's.

"See one of your friends is going away," Josh said.

"She's going to do some shopping."

"At the county seat?" Josh asked.

"In the city."

Asa thrust a pile of mail at me. There was a long white envelope addressed to Sally, a bunch of circulars, and a note from Mrs. George. That surprised me because I wouldn't have expected her to write so soon after I'd been to see her.

Martha Renner's eyes followed me as I stepped out into the misty wind.

I got into the Volkswagen, and Timothy started up and pulled away, heading for the turn-off to Point Janeway.

I opened my letter. Mrs. George's spidery familiar hand, all round and smooth, jumped at me from the page.

Mary Ellen, dear, she wrote, I am so embarrassed. In the excitement of seeing you I forgot to mention that a man was by looking for you. He didn't leave his name, or state his business. I'm not sure, but I think it was just a little bit after you moved out, a day or two maybe. Has he found you? Is everything all right? Should I tell Juney that you'll be coming back soon? I'm sorry I forgot. It's awful to get old, I guess. He said it wasn't important anyhow. Maybe he was a salesman or something. Write me soon.

I read the letter through twice. Poor Mrs. George. I knew how angry she got with herself when she found her memory failing her. But this couldn't be important, I reasoned. There was no one who would be looking for me. And no one had come to the house to see me. She must be right. It was a salesman. And he wouldn't be likely to come all the way to Point Janeway to sell whatever he had to offer.

As I folded the letter away, I dropped the rest of the mail. Sally's long envelope fell on top of it. I gathered the circulars up, and at the same time I noticed the return address on her letter. It said, *Bureau of Prisons, Department of Parole*. I covered it quickly, hoping Timothy's attention was fixed on the road, and that he hadn't noticed. Now I knew at least a part of Sally's secret, but I had no intention of revealing it.

When we got back to Point Janeway, I hurried up to our room, and put the letter into Sally's top dresser drawer.

She returned before dinner, carrying a small bag of purchases from the dime store. "I decided," she said, smiling happily, "to go easy on the spending bit. I mean, if I'm ever going to get myself to San Juan, then I need to save my money."

I pulled a heavy sweater over my head, then brushed casually at my hair with my fingers. I saw her reach toward the top dresser drawer. I said quickly, "Sally, there's a letter for you there." I added, "Nobody knows about it but me."

Her face turned red and then white. Her hand shook as she took the envelope from the drawer, murmuring, "They said they'd sent the notice. Just because I was a day or two late. They said . . . but I was hoping. . . ." Her voice broke. Her blue eyes filled with tears. "It was such a dumb thing to do, Mary Ellen. I . . . I wanted it so bad. And I didn't have the money. A lizard bag."

"Never mind," I told her. "Forget about it. Nobody knows but me, and I won't tell."

She sagged to the edge of the bed. "It was so awful, you see. Ten months of it. Being caged up. I had to go in a couple of days ago, and I didn't. But it won't happen again. I promised. I'll report every month. Just the way I'm supposed to."

"It'll be all right," I assured her.

"You won't tell the rest of them," she begged. "If they knew. . . ."

"They wouldn't care, Sally."

I was sure that they wouldn't. Barney had his own secret. And then there was Anne. I couldn't imagine Hester or James or Timothy turning against her either.

"But suppose they did, Mary Ellen. Suppose they told me I had to go?"

"They won't know about it, Sally."

She swallowed hard. "Thank you, Mary Ellen. Somehow I believe you. I trust you. I know you won't tell."

A gray dawn filled the room.

The house was still, but somewhere a floor board creaked.

I supposed that was what had awakened me so early.

I stretched and sighed, turned over and nestled beneath the heavy quilts for warmth.

It was a moment before I realized that Sally's quilts were thrown back. Her bed was empty. She was gone.

Her robe and her slippers were gone, too.

I sat up, listening hard. I told myself that she must have gone down the ball to the bathroom. I told myself that she was all right. But I remembered how upset she had been before she went to bed, before she had begun to accept my reassurances.

My heart began to pound against my ribs.

My throat began to tighten.

I got up, pulled on my terry cloth robe. I stuck my feet into sneakers, and went into the hall.

From where I stood, I could see that the bathroom door was open. It was empty. No one was there.

I hurried down the front stairs, went quickly from room to room.

I found her in the kitchen.

Her small plump body was sprawled beneath the open door of the oven. Her face was a bright pink.

A pink as bright as the pillow I had made for Kelly's head . . . I remembered how it lay on the tangled velvet throw the night he died.

Sally lay terribly still.

A bitter acrid cloud choked my breath away.

I screamed and ran for the door.

8

BARNEY caught me, held me. "What's going on?" he demanded, his voice harsh with suspicion. "What's the matter with you?"

I remembered Carlotta's hysterical voice, her accusing eyes.

I choked for breath on the acrid cloud.

Before I could find words and air with which to answer him, Barney saw Sally's limp body. He recognized the acrid cloud as gas.

With a curse, he thrust me aside. He raced for the kitchen door and flung it open. He threw open the two windows. He grabbed up Sally and carried her outside.

It happened so quickly that it seemed a blur before my eyes, his movements run off on a film at high speed.

It was Glencarlyn, jumping the kitchen steps, who caught me as I collapsed. Glencarlyn carried me into the fresh misty air where I could breathe again.

It was he who held me while I stammered out what had happened.

By then, the others had heard the commotion and come running from their bedrooms.

They were standing behind me when Barney straightened up and fumbled with his beard, muttering, "She's dead."

Anne cried, "But why? Why would she do a thing like that?" and put into the words the question that I knew we must all be asking ourselves.

I shook my head, thinking of the envelope, of what Sally had told me. I had promised to keep her secret in life. It seemed to me that I must keep it in death.

"But you were closest to her," Barney said. "You've got to have some idea. This thing, it just blows my mind. I'm not able to take it. Why should she kill herself?"

Why? She had promised she would never miss reporting to the parole people again. She had trusted me not to reveal her secret. Then why?

It never occurred to me then that Sally's death could be anything but suicide. How else could she have died in a kitchen full of gas, with the jets all turned on, and the windows and doors closed? But I still couldn't understand why she had done it.

Hester said slowly, "I guess we'll never know the truth."

Glencarlyn called the state police.

They came hours later, bringing with them the doctor who declared Sally's death self-inflicted while of unsound mind.

They questioned us, and filled out forms and went back to the county seat forty miles away, satisfied that they had done their jobs.

Sally had no relatives to notify.

We buried her in the small old cemetery in Stony Ridge.

I packed her things away, and secretly wrote a letter to the Parole Department, telling them what had happened. I burned the letter Sally had had from them, without reading it, and then I packed her things and put them into the attic.

Glencarlyn helped me. He said, "It's sad, Mary Ellen. She was so young. She had so much to live for."

I nodded, choking back tears.

Sally wouldn't be able to go to San Juan now, seeking her fresh start.

Sally had said, "One less is one less.

And that means there'd be more for the rest of us."

There was one less now. There would be more for the rest of us, I suppose. But Sally wouldn't share in it.

"And you really have no idea why she did it?" Glencarlyn asked.

I shook my head.

But I asked myself once again, as I had so often in the past three days, whether Sally had been so fearful of being found out that she had taken her own life. I asked myself if my accidental discovery of her secret had driven her to it.

Glencarlyn said, "It can't have anything to do with Point Janeway, you know."

"I don't see how it could," I agreed.

His blue eyes were thoughtful. "But that would mean there was something in her past, something behind her."

A shiver touched me. I thought of Barney, and Anne. But only Sally was dead.

A shiver touched me. Why was Glencarlyn dwelling on it?

"But what could it have been?" I asked hastily.

"That's what I keep wondering," he answered.

It was Barney who notified the bank. He said, one sunny morning, "Our checks are due in a week, aren't they? We'd better do something about Sally's."

Timothy agreed. "Yes, that's right. I never even considered that. What do you suppose will happen?"

"Nothing will," Hester said.

Barney smiled sourly in his black beard. "I know one thing that will. Our checks will be larger."

"Yes," Anne agreed.

"We don't know that for sure," James objected.

Barney explained as if he were speaking to a child. "In words of one syllable, James. There were seven of us sharing in the estate, and in the house. Now there are six."

I could hear Sally again, her breathless giggle, "There'd be more for us if you pull out, Timothy."

James sighed. "I'd sooner we were still seven, old chap."

"But we aren't," Barney retorted. "And we can't do anything about that."

I thought of Gentry Carrier's disappearance. He couldn't tell me about my benefactor now. He couldn't tell me about Sally either. He couldn't answer any of my questions. But, as Barney had said, the bank would take care of the change resulting from Sally's death. And we would all benefit by it.

I didn't like the thought. It touched me with an inner cold.

I felt Glencarlyn's quizzical blue gaze, and the inner cold grew stronger.

"Only she won't be going to San Juan after all," Timothy said softly. "That's what bothers me. That Sally won't be getting to go. It was such a dream with her."

I pushed away my coffee cup, unable to drink any more. I had to get away from the others.

I went up to my room, a room that seemed terribly empty in Sally's absence. I took a heavy sweater, and went down the back stairs.

Hester spoke to me as I crossed the

kitchen. I just shook my head, hurried outside.

The wind was strong, cold. The sun was too bright suddenly, too clear.

I took deep steadying gulps of the cold air as I followed the path down the ridge.

Glencarlyn angled out of the wind-warped trees and fell into step beside me. He said, "That talk at breakfast got to you, didn't it, Mary Ellen?"

I nodded.

"It's always like that after a death," he said gently. "You know that it is. Somebody has to pick up the pieces."

"Yes, but . . . but somehow . . ." I couldn't go on. I found myself thinking of Kelly, about when he died. Carlotta's raw angry voice accusing me until her husband led her away. Accusing me: "You did it. You! You can't fool me with your big blue eyes! I know you did it. You killed him!" And Jim Henry's quiet soothing, "She didn't mean it, Mary Ellen. It's shock. Hysteria!"

But Kelly had been an old man. She must have realized that sooner or later he would die. Die as naturally and easily as his doctor had said. Why had she accused me? What had I done? She had left him, she said, well, laughing, himself. But she had shrilled at him angrily. I had heard her voice and run away from it. And why did I keep remembering the pink pillow on the tangled velvet throw? Jim Henry had said, "I want you to forget it, Mary Ellen. I'll give you a bonus. It will help you make a new start somewhere else." I'd refused the bonus. I'd moved in with Mrs. George. I'd set out to find a job. But bad luck had dogged me. Every one I'd applied for, with my good references from the Henrys, had fallen through.

And then came the letter from Gentry Carrier. . . .

Glencarlyn was saying, "But somehow it bothers you. Sally. Is that it?"

I said, "I suppose so," and stumbled.

He caught my arm to steady me, and for just a moment I leaned against him.

I felt his strength, the rock hardness of his body. I felt a peculiar surge of pleasure. I pulled away quickly.

He didn't seem to notice. He held my arm until I freed myself and went ahead to the quarry rim. I sat on a big rock and peered into the bottomless green water that rippled far below.

Glencarlyn sat down beside me. "It has a certain fascination, hasn't it?"

"Yes. Ever since I first saw it I've felt that."

"Hester's scared of the place. I suggested a walk down the other day, and she said she'd seen it once and once was enough."

I smiled. "Yes. I know how she feels." I was remembering when we had been at the quarry rim together, and the two wedding rings on the chain at her throat. "It *is* a little scary, I guess."

"And should be. A slip from here. . . ." He stopped himself.

I knew that he had been going to say that a slip from where we sat would mean certain death, and he was suddenly remembering Sally again.

To change the subject I asked, "What are you working on?"

"What?"

"The book," I told him.

"Oh. Well, it's a novel. I haven't quite got it going. Maybe it'll be a love story."

"A love story? That's funny."

"Why? Why shouldn't I write a love story?" he demanded.

"I don't really know anything about such things," I told him, suddenly uncomfortable. "But you. I would have thought that you would be interested in . . ."

"In what?" he laughed.

His amusement annoyed me. I said, "How do I know what you should write? But I'd have thought . . . well, cops and robbers, and mysteries, and things like that."

He stared at me intently for a long silent moment. Then he threw back his head and laughed again. "I think you've seen too many television shows, Mary Ellen."

"What's that got to do with it?" I demanded.

"You're going by looks, aren't you? By surface clues? It's time you learned that looks don't mean a thing. And surface clues are merely masks. You mustn't believe everything you see, nor everything that you think you see. No matter what anyone tells you."

I looked away from the amusement in

his eyes. In an odd way, I sensed that he was warning me. But warning me of what?

He went on quickly, "For instance, you and your cousins—what do you really know about each other?"

I had thought the same thing before, I realized. I had wondered what we had in common, and how we came to be related. I had even wondered if we really *were* related. But we must be. We must. Else how could we share in an inheritance? That led me back to Gentry Carrier again. Where had he gone? What did his disappearance mean? Why was I so reluctant to tell the others what I had learned?

"Yes," Glencarlyn said, repeating himself. "Just what do you know about your cousins?"

I didn't answer him. I knew that we were each of us quite alone in the world. I knew that we had been all at loose ends when we heard from Gentry Carrier. I knew that at least three of us had had something to hide.

Glencarlyn went on after a moment, "Mary Ellen, I'm curious. How did you come to decide on occupying Point Janeway yourselves? Why didn't you just sell it, and take your shares, and go your own ways?"

I glanced at him, wondering at the question.

"It's not a secret affair, is it?" he asked quickly.

"No. It's not a secret affair. The lawyer said the house wasn't salable. And if you'd seen it when we first came, you'd understand."

"I still do," he told me.

I nodded. "So we . . . . well, we thought if we lived rent free, together, then we'd have more. And none of us had anything to hold us in the city. So that's what we did. And . . . and it's worked out."

He gave me another long intent look. Then, "And you're comfortable here? You're content?"

"I suppose so," I said uneasily.

"Except for what happened to Sally, I mean."

"Well, yes, except for that," I agreed reluctantly.

"Have you thought much about the future?"

"No. Not really."

"But why? You're twenty-two." He

paused. Then, "You are about that, aren't you? Isn't it time for you to think ahead?"

"I don't know," I answered. Then, "Yes, yes, you're right. I know I should. But just for a little while, being here. . . ."

"Is that what Point Janeway is to you? A way station?"

"Of course. What else? I don't plan to stay here forever. None of us do."

"Then when are you leaving?" The question was abrupt, urgent, cold.

I snapped, "I don't know. I haven't thought about it yet."

"That's what you just told me," he said soberly. "And what I'm telling you is that it's time for you to be thinking about it."

"I don't think it's any of your business, Glencarlyn."

"No," he agreed, suddenly laughing. "No. It's not. But I have a funny way, Mary Ellen. When things bother me I just make them my business."

"All right. What about you then?" I demanded. "You said you'd be staying a month. It will be behind you soon. Where are you going from here? What will you do?"

"I don't know yet either," he confessed.

"Would you believe me if I told you that I'm just as confused as you are?"

I looked into the quarry. A streak of sunlight made a glowing path across it. "I'll refer you to what you said before. That I accept the masks people wear. And that goes for you, too."

But I had unspoken reservations. I had begun to wonder now about Glencarlyn. I just didn't believe that he was a man who busied himself writing love stories. I didn't believe he was a man who didn't know where he was going. Instinct, built up over long years of being alone, of assessing strangers, told me that Glencarlyn was not entirely what he seemed, what he wanted to seem.

I realized suddenly that while I was now busy assessing him, I had from the very begininng uncritically accepted the others. Barney was a draft evader. Anne had been accused of involvement in some sort of confidence game. Sally had been a shoplifter. I had known nothing about them until accident revealed the truth as far as the girls were concerned, and confession as far as Barney. What about the others, Hester and James and Timothy?

Glencarlyn said, "Now you take Timothy. . . ."

I was speechless with surprise. I felt as if Glencarlyn had actually looked into my mind.

Finally I gathered myself together, asked, "What about him?"

Glencarlyn grinned, "That high-class family of his. The Jordans that he's always talking about."

"But they're all dead, you see."

"Or they never lived at all," Glencarlyn told me. "Except in his fantasies."

"What?"

"Didn't you ever wonder? Does he seem like the scion of a family like that?"

"I never thought of it. . . . He spoke of them, and Sally. . . ." My voice broke. I took a deep breath, went on, "Sally kidded him, saying he couldn't be part of that family because then how could he be an heir of Ralph Dartmoor's, and he said the family was all dead. I believed him."

"And you still do?"

"It doesn't matter, does it?"

Glencarlyn shrugged. "I don't know. But I'm curious, Writers are always curious."

"Then ask him."

"The truth is, I'd rather you did, Mary Ellen."

"But why should I?" I demanded. "I don't care about his precious family."

Glencarlyn was quiet for a moment. Then, "Well, maybe you ought to."

I brushed the words aside, changed the subject. Timothy and his family, or lack of it, were none of Glencarlyn's business, I decided. He had no right to involve himself with us. He was a stranger, passing through. Within a short time he would be gone.

But his question stayed with me.

Was Timothy's talk of his family a pretense? Was he hiding something, too? Could that something help me discover the truth about our joint inheritance?

That afternoon he walked me into Stony Ridge.

He waited outside while I bought a few things, picked up the mail.

When I rejoined him, I said, "No mail for you, Timothy."

He grunted. "There never is. Except the check."

"If Mrs. George didn't write to me once

a week there'd never be anything for me either," I answered.

He shrugged. He took the packages from me, hugged them to his plump chest, and started out the highway. I had to hurry to keep up with him. "It's funny," I said. "Except for you, because at least you did have your family, we're all of us in the same boat. I mean none of us has any background at all."

He flushed. He didn't answer.

"Not that it matters," I said quickly. "But it gives us something in common."

"It does," he agreed, blinking behind his glasses.

"At least you had the Jordans, and you belonged to them, but the rest of us . . ."

He said harshly, "Mary Ellen, I never did. You've figured it out, haven't you? I made it all up. There weren't any Jordans. There wasn't any big house with beamed ceilings, nor French windows. There wasn't anything but a . . . an orphanage."

"That's true of me as well as you," I told him. "But why? why did you . . ."

"Daydreams," he said briefly. "I got tired of being nobody. I started it a long time ago. And it kept on, and grew, and

147

now . . . well, I don't mind telling you. I feel different now. I've got somebody. I belong. I don't need it any more."

I swallowed a quick lump in my throat. I said, "Then we really all are in the same boat, aren't we?" and thought how right Glencarlyn had been, and wondered how he had known, and why he had cared.

"You won't. . . ." Timothy shot me a sideways look, stopping under the warped trees. "Listen, Mary Ellen, it's kind of embarrassing. You I don't mind you knowing, but the others . . . well, I'd rather that they didn't know."

"I won't tell them. Not if you don't want me to."

He sighed in relief. "And I'll cut it out. Okay?"

I didn't know then how little our promises would mean.

9

IT was just two days later.

I heard the tapping of Glencarlyn's typewriter from his room down the hall as I buttoned my green woolen dress.

Judging by how long that tapping had been going on, he had been hard at work for hours. He seemed, finally, to have gotten going on his book, love story, or whatever it was.

Glencarlyn. . . . His name was a thoughtful whisper in my mind. A questioning whisper, too. How odd that he had turned up so soon after we'd come to Point Janeway . . . how easily he had ingratiated himself, stayed on.

I went to the mirror. Aquamarine eyes looked back at me, eyes strangely shadowed with doubt. Glencarlyn. . . . Why did he seem so intimately related to all of us? He was no more than a chance acquaintance, and yet. . . .

I shrugged and the chestnut hair rippled on my shoulders. It was longer than I was used to wearing it. I decided I'd soon go into the city, have a trim, visit with Mrs. George. It was a pleasant thought. I would escape Point Janeway for a little while.

I kept my eyes carefully away from the bed that had been Sally's as I left the room to go downstairs.

Anne and Hester had just finished setting the table for dinner.

Anne wore a white see-through blouse and white pants, Hester was in a pair of pink hot pants with tight black tights.

I covered my amusement at their obvious dressing up by lighting the flame under the beef stew that I had cooked earlier in the day. Then I set about making a salad.

My amusement deepened as Anne asked, "Is Glencarlyn still upstairs?" But, oddly, I found myself savagely tearing the lettuce to shreds.

I said, "I heard the typewriter going so I suppose that he is," and bent my head over the sink.

"My worst enemy," she chuckled. "Whoever thought I'd be jealous of a typewriter?"

"Me, too," Hester put in. "I can't see

the strange fascination that thing has for him."

"He's working," I told them both. "I guess that's fascinating."

I thought of Sally . . . the way she had watched him breathlessly.

"Never mind the work," Anne said. "What I wish is that he'd concentrate like that on me."

"Or me," Hester said, laughing.

Was it for Anne, for Hester, that he stayed on? The month he had specified in the beginning was very nearly over, but he'd made no mention of leaving. Was it because he returned the interest of one or another of these girls? Or did he have another reason?

My fingers tore the lettuce, slapped the shreds into a strainer. I felt a strange quiver inside me. Anne, with her slow exotic smile and lush good looks, and Hester with her pert ways and hot brown eyes, were competition I couldn't hope to beat. Even if I wanted to. And I didn't want to, I told myself severely. Let the two of them fight over blue-eyed Glencarlyn. I wouldn't.

Hester was laughing, "And he's enough

to make a girl change her mind. Marrying him . . ."

Anne said quickly, "You haven't been married, have you?"

I kept my head down. I could feel Hester looking at me. I knew she was remembering that I had seen the two wedding rings she wore on a chain around her neck. I knew she was wondering what I would say.

Finally though, she laughed, "Oh, sure." She paused. Then, "Not once, but twice. What of it?"

"Nothing," Anne said, as I let my rigid shoulders relax. "Nothing at all." She went on in a bright airy voice. "Except that if you've tried it twice and found it no good I'd think you'd be about ready to give up."

Hester's voice shook. "What do you mean? What are you implying?"

"Why, nothing, Hester," Anne answered. She moved in her slow, long-legged walk toward the kitchen steps. "I'll go up and see what's keeping Glencarlyn."

"That's so obvious," Hester purred. "Why don't you stop chasing the man?"

Anne turned back, green eyes narrowed

with malice. "And you? What do you need another man for when you've already had two husbands?"

I put the salad in the refrigerator to chill. It was time to break up that conversation, I told myself. I turned, forcing a laugh. "If the two of you could hear yourselves. . . . If Glencarlyn could hear you. . . ."

Anne grinned, swung up the stairway.

But Hester sat at the table, round red spots of anger glowing on her creamy cheeks, her brown eyes hot. "What does she know?" she said through thinned lips. Her hand slid to her throat, drew out the chain. Her fingers toyed with the two wedding rings. "She doesn't know. Of course not. How could she?" Brown eyes swung to me. "Quiet Mary Ellen. . . that's what Barney always calls you. It's supposed to be a joke, isn't it? But it's no joke. You didn't tell her about me."

I shook my head.

"It cooks inside. It keeps hurting. And it . . . it keeps scaring me, too," she went on in a whisper. "They haunt me . . . all of them. They hang around my neck. Just like these rings." She took off the chain, dropped it on the table. "Anne. . . . She wants Glencarlyn, but James—she's already got James. I have a right to start over again, haven't I?"

I didn't answer her. I knew she didn't expect me to.

"Yes," she whispered. "I was married twice. I had two children by the time I was eighteen. I walked out. I left them. I couldn't stand it any more. A couple of years ago, I got married again. It wasn't any good. So I walked out."

"I'm sorry," I told her. "I know divorce isn't easy, but . . ."

She smiled faintly. "Maybe it isn't. I wouldn't know. I never got one divorce, much less two."

"Hester," I gasped, "You can't mean . . ."

"But that's just what I mean," she said. "That's what scares me. Because it won't let me make a fresh start." Then she shrugged, picked up the chain and slipped it around her neck. "But I will," she said brightly. "Anne can't stop me. Nothing, nobody can. I will."

At that moment, Barney came in through the kitchen door. He rubbed his hands, stamped his boots. "Man, it's cold out there. I think there's a storm blowing in over the mountains."

"I think so, too," Hester agreed brightly.

"I stacked some wood in the fireplace. We'll be warm in here, no matter what happens outside," he told us.

Some time after dinner a storm blew up.

The house creaked and moaned under its onslaught. The windows rattled under pelting curtains of hail. The trees bent and swayed, their warped limbs scratching the walls, their final crop of dying leaves skimming across the roof slates. Ominous autumn thunder echoed in great drum rolls across the ridge.

But we were as warm as Barney had predicted. We gathered in the living room before the fireplace, comforted by the sight of the leaping flames.

Glencarlyn sprawled on the sofa, wrapped in a peculiar stillness, though his eyes seemed to move speculatively from one to another of us. Studying us, weighing us. Was this a writer's curiosity showing? Or was it something else?

Anne curled up next to him, long curved legs displayed by her tight pants.

James watched from an easy chair in the corner, his hands nervously plucking the crease in his tan trousers.

Timothy lay on the rug, a book open before him.

Barney and Hester were playing cards.

Hester, after a single beseeching look at me when Barney interrupted her confession, seemed to have put it behind her. A smile glowed on her face as she added the score.

Masks, Glencarlyn had said. We all wore masks.

How right he had been.

There was a pattern. I saw its outlines faintly.

There had been seven of us, each in our twenties, each without ties or known family. Now, there was another bond obscurely beginning to appear.

Barney was a draft evader.

Sally had been a shoplifter.

Anne had been accused, at least, of playing a confidence game.

Hester was, without ever using the word herself, a bigamist.

Timothy lied about his fantasy family, and was now ready to disown it. Had he made up the Jordans out of loneliness? Or had he another reason?

Masks . . . each one of them had memories, fears, to escape.

And what of James? He sat so quietly, watching Anne lean close to Glencarlyn. What did his thin face conceal? His not-quite real accent?

Even I wore a mask, I realized suddenly. Yes. Of course I did. I sat quietly, considering each of the others, pretending to them that I didn't know their secrets.

Thunder rolled over us. The flames danced in the fireplace.

Glencarlyn laughed at some low-voiced comment of Anne's.

I suspected that he, too, had something to conceal. Where had he come from? Why had he wanted to stay on? Who was the real Glencarlyn?

Chilled, uneasy, over-burdened with questions to which I had no answers, I decided to make coffee. I asked if the others wanted to join me. They agreed so enthusiastically that I wondered if they had shared my chill, if they had been asking themselves questions and were glad of an excuse to dismiss them.

I went into the kitchen and set up the percolator. It took a little time for the water to heat, but I sat at the table alone, waiting until it was ready. I set up a tray with seven cups and saucers, thinking of Sally again, and hurriedly took the creamer and sugar, and when the coffee was clear and dark, I carried it into the living room.

Everyone helped themselves.

Timothy had a cup, and then left us, saying he was going to bed.

Barney decided he wanted a snack, and went into the kitchen to fix it.

Glencarlyn went to see what the storm was like outside.

Anne decided to get some things from the attic to see if she could make them wearable.

Hester and I straightened up, and then went upstairs.

I don't know why every detail of that night was so firmly fixed in my mind. It seemed, then, no different from any other evening. But somehow I noted everyone's comings and goings. Somehow I remembered them later.

Once again it was the sound of Glencarlyn's typewriter that awakened me early.

The room was bright with sun.

Through the window I could see patches of blue sky laced with the dark warped limbs of the trees.

The storm was over, I saw with a lift of spirits. It was a beautiful day.

I dressed quickly, and went down to the kitchen.

I was the first one up, it seemed.

I made the coffee, had a quick glass of juice, and went out of doors.

It was cold, crisp. I took a few deep breaths, and then started down the slope toward the quarry.

I walked carefully, picking my way across the still damp rocks, and watching my footing.

I had gone only a short way from the house when I tripped on a shoe. I stopped, picked it up. I had never noticed it on the path before, though it was a walk I had made often, either alone or with one of the others. I turned the shoe in my suddenly shaking hand. It belonged to a man. It was soaked through. It had plainly been out all night in the storm.

Holding it, wondering whose it was, I went on.

My shadow moved before me, long and very dark on the damp stones. The path grew more steep, the rocky slope fell away. Below me I could see the white walls of the quarry, and the bottomless green water within it.

I stopped. I leaned against a boulder, turning the shoe nervously in my hands.

The sun seemed less bright now, and when I turned to look back at the house, it seemed to be floating on the ridge in a veil of mist.

It was when I rose to go back that I saw something twinkle a few feet away. A gleam of reflecting glass.

I stared at it, my heart suddenly beginning to pound. I knew then. I knew what I would find.

Yes, even before I scrambled off the path, I was certain of it. Praying to be in error, hopelessly praying, I tripped and fell and got up again. I kept going as fast as I could. It took me only moments. They were moments that seemed eons. Then I stood over the shiny glass, staring, wondering.

Timothy's glasses.

I squeezed the damp shoe, and picked up the glasses.

Yes. They were his, the frames bent, one lens shattered. But I knew they were Timothy's glasses.

I was frozen there, the cold wind icy on my cheeks, robbing me of breath and strength. Timothy's shoe, his glasses . . . I couldn't move.

"Hey, what're you doing down there?"

Those words, from above me, brought me back to myself.

Glencarlyn was down on his knees, balancing on a boulder above me. "What's the matter, Mary Ellen? Why did you get down off the path?"

I held up the shoe, the glasses.

He was a still, faceless silhouette for a moment. Then he turned, swung his legs into space, and lowered himself to full length from his fingertips. He let go and dropped to his feet. He scrambled across the rocks between us, and wordlessly looked at the shoe, the broken glasses.

"Timothy. . . ."

I nodded.

Glencarlyn's lips were narrow, expressionless, his eyes hooded. "Stay here," he ordered. He moved away, ducking beneath an overhanging shelf of granite.

I obeyed only momentarily, then I went after him.

I dodged the shelf and came out on the other side, and almost stumbled over him.

He was on his knees, next to Timothy's still body.

"Go back to the house," he told me.

But I stood there.

Timothy's wide-open eyes stared emptily at the blue sky. His shirt and trousers were wet under his wet jacket. He wore only one shoe. He looked young and defenseless, and curiously unmarked.

"But what . . . what is it?" I stammered. "What's the matter? Why doesn't he get up?"

I knew even then. I knew, but I didn't want to believe it.

Timothy. The fantasy family he had

given up. Timothy saying, "I don't need it any more. I belong to somebody now."

"Mary Ellen, go up to the house," Glencarlyn said tonelessly. "Go on. Get Barney for me."

"But . . . but what's wrong?" I insisted.

Glencarlyn rose. He put his arms around me. He held me briefly.

I accepted it then. I believed it finally.

I said, "He's dead, isn't he? Timothy's dead."

Glencarlyn said, "Yes, Mary Ellen, now go on. Do as I say."

But I knelt next to Timothy's still body. I saw the terrible wound at the back of his head, and the dark blood smeared on the rocks.

"He fell down," I cried. "He did fall down, didn't he? That's what it is, isn't it?"

Glencarlyn said soberly, "I think so, Mary Ellen. Now I want you to go inside."

We buried Timothy beside Sally in the Stony Ridge cemetery.

We went back to the house together, none of us quite able to look each other in the face.

Death had come to Point Janeway again.

First Sally.

Now Timothy.

Barney was prepared to deal with our unspoken thoughts. "Accidents happen," he said. "Listen. We can't let it get us down. I mean, I know it's enough to blow your mind all right. But look how it is. Sally, that was one thing. I mean, you know, she broke up. Something got her down. She finished herself off. Okay. But Timothy, now that was something else again. I mean, poor kid, he was just out for a walk, I guess."

He had said he was going to bed, I remembered. He'd had a cup of the coffee I made, and gotten up and yawned, and said he was going to bed. The book he'd been reading was tucked under his arm.

Barney was saying, "Like it's fate or something. He just went out for a walk. And I guess, in the storm, he lost his footing and had that fall, and that was it."

Anne said throatily, "It was just one of those things."

James plucked nervously at his tie. "Of course. Poor chap. What else?"

Hester sat very still, her small hands

folded in her lap, her creamy face expressionless.

We had called the state police again. Glencarlyn insisted that accidental deaths had to be reported as well as suicides.

The troopers had driven the forty miles from the county seat, and spent a little while checking the path, the rocks onto which Timothy had fallen. They asked us each a few questions, and then they had left.

The questions had remained behind, filling Point Janeway with an invisible mist.

First Sally.

Now Timothy.

There had been two deaths.

We had been seven at first, but now we were only five.

We were strangers who had come together because Ralph Dartmoor had made us his heirs, because we were all cousins of sorts.

Barney said that he would notify the bank of Timothy's death. There was nothing else to do. He didn't mention the fact that our five checks would be larger now. But we all knew they would be.

The mist of questions filled my mind as well as the house.

I was frightened now. We had been seven. Now we were five. Who would be next?

Were we all doomed? All seven of Ralph Dartmoor's heirs doomed to die in the house he had left us? Was that the fate in store for us, for me?

Had Sally committed suicide?

Had Timothy's death been an accident?

Or were we each slated to die? Until there was only one left?

When I packed Timothy's things for storage in the attic, I found the book he had been reading the night he died.

I held it, turned it in my fingers, wishing it could talk.

Had he returned to his room before he'd gone out into the storm, and left the book behind him?

Or had he carried it with him and dropped it so that it was found later by someone else.

I put the book with his clothes, and didn't mention it to the others.

10

JOSH RENNER peered at me over his glasses. "I see you got yourself another cousin out there," he said. "Come from a big family, don't you?"

I was surprised that he was willing to be conversational for a change. Neither he, nor Martha, nor Asa Whalen, had been anything more than short with me before. But I was even more surprised that he was so indirectly asking me about Glencarlyn after all this time. It was well past a month since he had appeared at Point Janeway. Josh had had plenty of time to question me about him.

Still, if Josh wanted to talk I was willing.

I smiled, shook out my hair. "I'm afraid I don't come from a family at all."

"If cousins aren't family, then what are they?" Martha put in suspiciously.

"I just don't know how we're related," I answered.

Josh's eyes narrowed above his glasses.

"Blood kin is blood kin. There's only the one kind."

"You know what I mean. I don't know through whom, or how, the connection can be made."

I could hardly blame the Renners for wondering, when I had wondered about the same thing myself.

Josh went on, "But you all moved in to Ralph Dartmoor's house together. And then he," Josh jerked his head toward the window through which he could see Glencarlyn in his long white car, "then he came along."

"Glencarlyn," I said. "But he's not a cousin. He's just staying with us."

"He had a hard enough time finding you. I'll say that for him. If you wanted him to come, then why didn't you give him decent directions?"

I stared at Josh, not sure that I understood, hoping that I didn't. "A hard time finding us?"

"That's just what I said."

"But he. . . ." I stopped suddenly.

The quick suspicion that swept me choked the words in my throat.

Glencarlyn was outside, waiting for me.

I had planned to walk in to Stony Ridge, but he had insisted that it was too cold.

He had been with us something over a month, and in that time both Sally and Timothy had died.

He had come upon the house, upon us, accidentally, he had said, and asked to be allowed to stay so that he could write his book. Until then, nothing had happened. Nothing. Nothing.

And since then. . . .

Who was he?

What did he want?

Why had he asked for directions to Point Janeway?

Josh demanded triumphantly, "What's the matter? You look like you've been struck by lightning."

I forced a smile, "Not exactly."

"I wouldn't think, if I was you, I'd stay around that place any more," Asa observed from behind the mail table. "Not me. I'd look for a safer spot to rest my bones."

Josh glanced at him sideways, shook his grizzled head.

"It's true," Martha put in. "That's a dangerous place, isn't it?"

Sally. . . .

Timothy. . . .

A shiver went over me.

And Glencarlyn had deliberately sought us out.

Was that why Sally had committed suicide?

Was that why Timothy . . . ?

But Timothy's death was an accident. He had gone out into the storm, and lost his way, and wandered off the path onto the treacherous rocks.

I shuddered, seeing the pool of blood under his head, his empty eyes staring at the sky.

What could Glencarlyn have had to do with either death?

What was I thinking?

"People," Josh observed, "don't like to talk about dying. Specially young people. And why should they? So I wasn't about to bring it up. But I do believe that Asa's right. If you had any sense, which I suppose some of you do, and some of you don't, you'd just sell out, and move on."

"But that's the trouble," I said. "Don't you see? We can't sell Point Janeway."

"You can't? There a lien on it I don't know about?"

"A lien?"

"Something wrong with the title. Money owed. That kind of thing," Josh explained, plainly watching my face as if prepared to trap me in a lie.

"Oh, no. It's nothing like that. It's just that nobody would want it," I explained. "That's what our lawyer told us. And since it couldn't be sold, we decided to move in and fix it up. And maybe some time. . . ."

Josh stared at me silently for a moment. Then he said, "I call that pretty peculiar. I do."

"What? Why?"

"Because Ralph Dartmoor's house was sold just three and a half months ago. That's why. And if somebody wanted it then I don't see why somebody wouldn't want it now."

"Three and a half months ago?" I echoed. "I don't understand."

"Looks like neither of us do," Josh answered.

"Ralph Dartmoor's been dead for four years, hasn't he?" I asked.

Josh nodded. "That's right. Four years. Left the house, and nothing else. And nobody to claim either one."

"But I don't see . . . I thought. . . ."

"Then somebody bought it. By mail. And for a song."

"Who got the money?"

Josh shrugged. "Ask the state. Not me."

Something was wrong. Only Gentry Carrier could explain it. But I didn't know where he was.

As casually as I could, I said, "I guess there's a mix-up."

I gathered my packages, nodded good-bye, and went out to the car.

Glencarlyn grinned. "Seems as if you're getting to be on pretty friendly terms with the folks in there."

"I was just visiting a little," I told him. "It's just about the first time they've seemed receptive so I feel that I'm making progress."

I wanted to blurt out everything that Josh had just told me, all the confusing bits of information. I wanted to accuse Glencarlyn of having sought us out at

Point Janeway deliberately, for some purpose not evident to me.

But it seemed more politic, and safer, too, somehow, to say nothing at the moment. I had to think, consider.

The house had been bought by someone unknown not many months before.

The people of Stony Ridge believed that Ralph Dartmoor had had no heirs.

Why would Gentry Carrier have invented a fictitious inheritance? Why would he have sought out the seven of us, brought us together? Why had he now disappeared?

Glencarlyn started the car moving, heading back to the turn-off. Then he said, "You're very quiet, Mary Ellen."

I sighed, folded my hands in my lap.

"I guess you're thinking about Timothy. He always drove you in." Glencarlyn waited. When I didn't respond, he went on, "I know it's hard. But remember, none of you were really close. You're just about strangers."

I had thought the same myself, and often. But hearing it from him, from him of all people, annoyed me.

I said, "You know that we're cousins."

"Are you?" he asked soberly.

I hesitated. Then, "I'm not sure actually. The lawyer wasn't very explicit."

"And you don't think that odd?" he asked.

"Yes," I snapped. "I have thought it odd. But what can I do about it?"

"You might consider, Mary Ellen, that one odd thing can lead to another."

I turned in my seat. I gave him a long deliberate stare.

He kept his eyes on the road, his profile hard and stern and ungiving. As ungiving as the rocks on which Timothy had died.

I said, "You're speaking in riddles. I don't like them. If you have something to say, then say it straight out."

He smiled faintly, "Sorry, Mary Ellen."

But I noticed that he didn't explain.

"I don't like riddles so much that I'm going to ask you a question. What are you doing at Point Janeway, Glencarlyn?"

The car skipped into a pothole and jolted. I banged into the dashboard. The wheel spun in his hands.

He swore softly, fighting for control.

It was only when we had skidded on to firm ground that he answered, "You know

174

perfectly well what I'm doing, Mary Ellen. I'm writing a book. A love story. I'm . . .''

I cut in, "Josh Renner just told me that you were asking directions to the house. He wanted to know why, if we expected you, we hadn't told you how to get there. He wanted to know if you're another cousin.''

"Josh Renner did?''

Glencarlyn was obviously stalling.

I said nothing, allowing the silence to lengthen between us.

At last he grinned, "That's a pretty nosy old man, isn't it?''

"I expect he's grown interested in us.''

"I expect he always was,'' Glencarlyn retorted. Then he went on, "I wonder why he's trying to stir things up.''

I shrugged. I knew why. Josh Renner had taken note of the two deaths at Point Janeway. He had begun to suspect Glencarlyn, too. Then I asked myself, but of what did he suspect Glencarlyn? Of what did I?

"Maybe he wants to buy the house, but wants it cheap.''

"He could have bought it before. When it was up for sale three months ago.''

The car jerked and swerved. Glencarlyn swore, and pulled it back on the road. Then he turned to me, "What was that? What did you say about the house?"

I bit my lip. I hadn't intended to tell him. But it had just slipped out. Now I was stuck with it. I said slowly, carefully, "Josh told me that the house was purchased just a few months ago from Ralph Dartmoor's estate."

"By whom?"

"Josh didn't know."

"Why did he mention that to you, Mary Ellen?"

"He was saying we should all sell and leave. I think he . . . well, Sally and Timothy . . . I think he was warning me in a way." Swallowing hard, I forced myself to go on, "And maybe, just maybe, that wasn't the reason. You know we're not very welcome around here somehow."

"I've noticed that nobody but you ever goes into town."

"The others . . . well, I guess the Renners and Asa Whalen make them feel uncomfortable."

"But doesn't it bother you?"

"Of course it does. What do you think? That I have no feelings?"

He smiled faintly again. "No, Mary Ellen. I don't think that you have no feelings. But you're willing to come in, to face the hostility you're talking about."

"Somebody has to shop. We all have to eat."

He glanced at me briefly, his eyes very blue in his tan, weathered face. "Why don't you tell me the truth, Mary Ellen. You want to break that hostility down, don't you? You want those old people to like you. You want to prove to them that you're a good sweet girl who . . ."

"What if I do?" I demanded. "And why are you making fun of me?"

"I'm not," he said soberly. "At least not by intention."

I saw how neatly he had managed to leave far behind the question I had asked him. He hadn't explained why he had been asking directions to Point Janeway. He hadn't told me why he had sought out the house, sought out the seven of us.

I tightened my hands in my lap. I took a deep breath. Then I asked, "Glencarlyn,

I want to know the truth. Why did you come to Point Janeway?"

He hesitated. Then, "Mary Ellen, Josh Renner is an old man. He didn't quite understand me, I guess. It's true I asked directions to Point Janeway. But only because I'd seen the ridge on the map, and I couldn't find the turn-off for it. So I stopped in at the store to find out where it was. But I was talking about the ridge. Not about the house. I didn't know about the house until I ran into Anne at the quarry."

His voice was steady, harsh, persuasive. He gave me a single quick straight look, then concentrated on the road again.

By all rights I should have believed him. Perhaps, in the beginning, I would have. But now I didn't. I couldn't. I knew Josh Renner too well. Old or not, he had all his wits about him. He knew what kind of a question he had been asked. He could remember and report it correctly. And one thing more. He wasn't a man to waste words. He didn't believe in idle conversation. He had deliberately told me about Glencarlyn, deliberately warned me.

Glencarlyn was lying to me.

I wondered why.

I wondered what he had to do with the seven of us, or with one of us. I wondered why he had come to Point Janeway to stay.

All along I had had the feeling that something was wrong. I couldn't quite believe that I was really entitled to an inheritance. I began to see now how improbable it was that the seven of us were really related, really bona fide heirs of Ralph Dartmoor. If we were not, then what had been the purpose of the deception that had brought us together?

I tried to think how, exactly who, had suggested that we live together. I recalled the lounge in which we had sat together, laughing, drinking to our good fortune. I remembered the waitress with long blonde hair and a green outfit. I remembered Barney's pale watered-ink blue eyes, and James' nervous hands, and Sally's joyful giggle. I could picture the flush on Timothy's face, and Anne's slow smile, and Hester's pert grin. But who had made the suggestion, or when, or how, evaded me.

Somehow it had been decided that we would join our fortunes, what small fortunes we had, and our futures, together. We had come to live in Point Janeway.

Now Sally and Timothy were dead.

Sally by her own hand, I reminded myself. And Timothy in a weird accident.

It was a sad and useless attempt to reassure myself, to hold back swift currents of fear.

The apparent facts of the two deaths were meaningless.

Sally had turned her back on her past, was ready to face the future. She had not planned to die.

Timothy had not gone out to walk in the storm when he'd left us that night. He'd gone to his room. The book that he'd put there proved it.

I gripped my fingers more tightly together.

The word for what I was thinking was murder.

We had all been brought together for some purpose I didn't understand. And now there were only five of us left.

"I think," Anne said, "that Hester's mad at me."

"Oh, why?" I asked.

"We were talking, just casually. You know how it is. And I asked her how come she didn't get alimony from her husbands. A smart girl manages to get some, you know." Anne grinned. "Maybe she thought I was implying that she wasn't smart. But she got red in the face. So red that I thought she was going to burst."

"Maybe she doesn't like to think about it," I told Anne. But I imagined that Hester suspected Anne was questioning her because of suspicion. I had the feeling Hester might think that I had given her secret away. I decided I would reassure her at the first opportunity.

Anne went on, "Anyhow, if you ask me, there's something funny about it, about her and her two divorces."

I didn't say anything.

"I'll bet there's a story behind it."

I knew that if Anne had given Hester even a hint of how strong her suspicions were, Hester would be terrified. I asked, "Where's Hester now?"

"She went stamping and fuming out.

For a walk," Anne answered. "At least that's what she said."

"Alone?" I asked uneasily.

"I guess so." Anne grinned again. "And if she knew that you and Glencarlyn were back she'd be grinding her teeth. She'd like to make that man number three and no mistake about it."

I went out into the hall.

The house was still, but from upstairs I heard the steady tapping of Glencarlyn's typewriter.

I wished I could read what he had written so far. I decided that the first time I had a chance to, perhaps when I was vacuuming, I would make sure to do it alone, and get a good look at his room.

Barney came stamping down the steps. "Want to go for a walk?"

I agreed that I would.

"See if you can find Hester," Anne said. "Tell her to come home. That all's forgiven."

I would, as soon as I could speak to her alone, tell Hester not to worry, that Anne knew nothing of which Hester need be afraid.

Aloud, I laughingly agreed to give her Anne's message, not knowing then that it would be impossible to tell Hester anything any more.

11

BARNEY and I picked our way down the path through the warped black trees.

He looked more like a pirate than ever with his long dark hair blowing over his shoulders and his black beard and the gold loop dangling from his ear.

We stopped at a point not far from where Timothy had fallen. I tried to keep my eyes away from the boulder where Glencarlyn and I had found him, but they sought it out in search of answers that were not there.

Barney's thoughtful voice reclaimed my attention. "Anne *did* say Hester had come down here, didn't she?"

I nodded, suddenly uneasy.

Why hadn't we met her, heard her?

Barney went on until he had made the last curve in the path. I followed in his footsteps.

The quarry was below us, white rock

walls rising straight and steep, green water still and bottomless.

He climbed down, stood at the rim, peering across the distance to the other side, his lips pursed in a soundless whistle.

On that wall there were long brownish streaks, gouges, and scored places.

They were new, fresh. I had never seen them before.

It was suddenly cold in spite of the sun.

I felt a deep shiver of dread.

Barney slanted a pale blue look at me, and for a fleeting instant a shock of unidentifiable recognition arose in me. It was submerged when he whispered hoarsely, "Do you see what I see?" And then his hand closed around my arm, holding me tightly, "Mary Ellen, something's wrong over there."

Hester. . . .

But she wouldn't have come to the quarry. She had always disliked, avoided it.

"It might be a rock slide," I said quietly. "Or maybe an animal."

"We'd better find her. Hester, I mean. Like quick, too."

Hester! I pulled away from Barney. I

moved closer to the rim. I filled my lungs with air and shouted, "Hester! Where are you? Hester, tell us. Where are you?"

My voice shrilled out across the quarry, and slowly came echoing back.

Barney yelled, too, roaring Hester's name into the stillness.

There was no answer, no pert reply, no acknowledgment of our fear.

But James and Anne came down the path together, arms linked as if clinging for strength.

"What is it?" James asked. "Why are you shouting? We heard you all the way back to the house."

"Over there," Barney said, pointing again.

"But what? I don't understand." Anne's husky voice was suddenly hard. "What does that mean? Why are you standing here and yelling for Hester like that?"

There was a sudden pallor in James' thin face. He said, "We had better get help, Barney."

"Put in a call," Barney ordered.

But none of us moved. Perhaps, like me, they couldn't. Perhaps they, too, were compelled to stand at the quarry rim and stare down into the cold green water.

Then Anne suddenly collapsed on to the rocks, moaning.

"That won't help," James said. "And besides, we don't know."

I looked at him, then at Barney.

Neither of them met my glance.

I bent over Anne, drew her to her feet. I knew she was remembering how she had teased Hester, how Hester had gone slamming out. I said, "This won't help. Let's go back to the house."

But she broke away from me, crying hoarsely, "We have to do something. We can't just stand here, can't pretend. . . . It's happened. It's happened again!"

"We don't know," Barney said quietly. "Maybe it's . . . well, you know, she could have just decided to walk in to Stony Ridge. Or. . . ."

My eyes went to the fresh gouges on the wall across from us, to the new brownish stains.

The sun was just beginning to set. The green water was dyed a strange and terrible red.

"We'd better make a search," James said.

And I thought of Glencarlyn. Where was he? Why hadn't he come down? If the others, if Anne and James, had heard our shouts, then why hadn't Glencarlyn come down?

I turned and ran for the house, leaving the others at the quarry edge.

I raced up the path, stumbling on the rocks, falling and getting up again. I burst out of the trees and into the sun-red clearing, shouting Glencarlyn's name.

The window of his room flew up. He leaned out. "What's the matter, Mary Ellen?"

Relief, turning my blood to water, my muscles to mud, made me realize that I had not expected him to answer. I had not thought he would be in the house. I swept the sudden understanding aside, and cried, "We can't find Hester. I don't know what's wrong. But we can't find her. Anne said she'd gone for a walk, and Barney and I went to look for her. But she's not . . ."

"I'll be down," Glencarlyn said. He disappeared from the window, leaving it open, its white curtain blowing out on the wind, like the white curtain of the sanctuary I had left behind in Mrs. George's cottage.

In a moment he was beside me. "All right. What really makes you think something's wrong?"

I told him about the scars on the quarry walls.

His mouth tightened. His blue eyes shifted away from mine. He turned toward the path down the slope.

I hung back, thinking of his now-empty room. Hester had disappeared, and I had thought Glencarlyn would be gone, too. I said, "I'm going to get something warmer for Anne and me."

He nodded without speaking and set out across the clearing, moving quickly with a hawk's arrogant grace.

From the distance, through the sunset-stained trees, I could hear James and Barney. They were shouting Hester's name again.

I hurried upstairs. First I went into Anne's room for a warm black shawl, then into mine for a pullover. From there I went into Glencarlyn's room. I had almost expected it to be locked. But the door hung open.

The typewriter was on a bridge table, a piece of paper under the roller.

I bent to look at what he had written.

The words didn't make sense. They were a jumble, a scattering of letters that added up to nothing. He had typed on the same sheet over and over again.

So this was his love story. This was his novel. He sat here, hour after hour, tapping out meaningless phrases.

He had left the typewriter hurriedly, too, forgetting to hide this revealing sheet in his haste.

If he wasn't a writer, then what was he?

Who was he?

What did he want?

Why had he come to Point Janeway?

I left the sheet where it was. Later, I told myself. Later I would think of what this discovery meant. Now I must think only of Hester.

I went down the front stairs to the foyer. The phone was on a small dull antique table which should have been beautiful but was only drab. Drab like everything in the house.

I called the state police, and then went down to the quarry.

The others had made their way to the opposite side. I went after them, slowly picking a path along the crumbly edge.

I was half way around it when I heard Glencarlyn's wordless shout.

His tall lean body was silhouetted against the pink twilight of the sky. He was peering down.

I squinted into the shadowy water.

Something white seemed to glimmer just below its surface.

Anne screamed shrilly, and buried her face in James' shoulder.

Barney came stumbling toward me. "Ropes. I'll get them from the shed."

I nodded, hurried on to the others.

I tucked the shawl around Anne's trembling shoulders, and put on my own pullover, hoping for a warmth it didn't give me.

James said softly, "I can't tell just what it is, you know. But something *is* down there."

Glencarlyn didn't answer. He moved away. He began searching deliberately along the rim.

I couldn't tell what he was looking for. I watched his tall lean body, and asked myself why he had come to us in subterfuge and stayed on in deception.

Barney came panting back, heavy coils of hemp looped around his arm.

He and Glencarlyn worked quickly, securing it to a nearby tree stump. Then Glencarlyn stripped down to trousers, and knotted the rope around his waist.

I bit back an involuntary protest as I realized what he meant to do.

I held my breath as James and Barney eased him over the edge.

I watched, standing to one side, as he slid cautiously down the steep white wall. It was slow, so terribly slow.

James grunted. Barney swore. Their faces were wet with perspiration. Their shoulders sagged with strain.

The waiting was unexplainable pain as Glencarlyn's body sank further and further into the quarry.

At last, when it seemed impossible for the two men to hold on longer, Glencarlyn touched the water. He disappeared into its depths.

But I saw the trail he made. He left a

shadowy foamy wake from the wall to where there was the glimmer of moving white. He surfaced there, and raised his hand.

"Yes," James said softly.

"Hester," Anne moaned, burying her face in the black shawl.

I watched as Glencarlyn pulled at a weight I couldn't quite see, as he swam with it back to the wall. I watched until I saw him unknot the rope at his waist.

Then I couldn't stand it any more.

I closed my eyes against the failing twilight, against what I knew was to come.

I heard Barney's straining breath, and James' gasps.

I heard the sudden bump, followed by silence, and the slow drip of water.

I stumbled away into the rocks, to weep alone.

But terror went with me. Terror tracked me soundlessly through the growing shadows, whispered to me on the cold wind.

Once again the word for what I was thinking was murder. But now it was no longer in question. It was a certainty in my mind.

Sally.

Timothy.

Now Hester. . . .

We had been seven in the beginning. There were only four of us left.

I remembered that I had wondered if we had all been brought together for some purpose I didn't understand. Now I asked myself if one of us was determined to outlive the rest, to gain the whole inheritance for himself.

The pattern was clear, frightening. It seemed to me that one of us, one of the surviving four, must be a madman, determined that each of those dead must forfeit their lives for what they had done in the past. Was Sally dead because she had once stolen a purse? Or Timothy because he lied about his family? Or Hester because she was a child deserter and bigamist? Then what about Barney, the draft evader? And Anne? Was James concealing something about himself, too?

I went back in my mind to the night Sally died.

She had not been thinking of suicide then.

And Timothy, the night of the storm. . . .

Hester, hating and fearing the quarry, would not have gone walking there, and certainly not alone.

The word I was thinking of was murder.

I knew that one of us in Point Janeway had lured Sally into the kitchen on some pretext, and Timothy into the thunder-ridden night, and Hester to her death in the green water.

One of us . . . Barney, or Anne, or James. Or . . . yes, or Glencarlyn.

He wasn't a writer.

He had deliberately come here offering what seemed truths, but were no more than plausible lies.

And it was soon after his coming that the deaths had begun.

So soon after. . . .

I thought of his faintly smiling lips, his speculative blue eyes. I felt the same sinking of my heart that I had felt when I saw him disappear into the sunset-stained water of the quarry.

Now I heard movement in the rocks. I dried my tears, knowing that the only escape from terror would be in the discovery of the truth.

Glencarlyn came to meet me, answering my unspoken question. "I'm sorry, Mary Ellen. I couldn't revive her. She's gone."

He reached out to help me to the path.

I cringed away from his touch, his cold wet touch.

He said harshly, "Be careful, Mary Ellen. Be very careful now," and turned away.

The state police spent a long time at Point Janeway. They set up search lights around the quarry, and did what seemed to be an inch-by-inch search of its rim.

They questioned each of us, first separately, and then as a group.

It was obvious that they were dissatisfied. Three deaths in so short a time was three too many for their experienced minds to accept.

But at last they left us, stony-faced and trailing unspoken suspicions behind them.

We listened to their cars rumble away between the stone pillars. One of us, I thought, must be sighing with relief.

Then Barney laughed, "The suspicious

Establishment mind. Like things don't just happen. But they do. It blows your mind how they do sometimes."

No one spoke. No one answered him.

He went on, "Ugly things in those short-cropped pointy little heads. Oh, yes, indeed, very ugly things. But they can't prove them." He laughed deep in his throat. "How can they? When there's nothing to prove."

"Of course," James agreed, his light voice indignant. "What a thing to suggest, Barney. Naturally there's nothing to prove."

Anne made a strangled sound.

Barney said harshly, "They could see how it was. She must have gotten careless where she walked. The edge crumbled out from under her. Those gouges, and streaks . . . it was plain. She probably never even felt it when she hit the water."

Hester was buried two days later.

We five had avoided each other's eyes, but somehow stayed close to one another, perhaps seeking a comfort in company that we couldn't find alone.

That night after dinner, we settled down before the fireplace.

Anne said, looking at Glencarlyn, "I guess this isn't turning out to be exactly what you expected."

"No," he answered.

I remembered the gibberish he had spent hours tapping out on the typewriter, but I said nothing about it. If he wasn't a writer, then he was something else. If he had come here by design, rather than by accident, then he had his reasons.

I was determined to find out what they were.

Anne went on, "You're not planning to leave, are you?"

"No," Glencarlyn told her, smiling faintly.

She moved from the easy chair in which she had been sitting to the sofa where Glencarlyn was sprawled. She shifted close to him, then closer.

I saw James give her a long sour look.

Barney said, "I know it's hard to get it together. But you've got to figure it's fate. Just fate. That's how it goes. And now we've got to hang in there. Because we're the only ones left."

There had been seven of us, I thought again. Now there were four. And I asked myself which one would be next.

Glencarlyn rose, stretched. "What we need is a drink. What do you say?"

"I say I agreed," James told him. "A couple of drinks might help lighten the gloom."

"Mary Ellen?" Glencarlyn asked, looking at me.

"No thanks."

"Sure?"

"Yes. I'm quite sure."

Barney got to his feet. "Don't listen to her. This chick is the kind that always says no. She doesn't know what's good for her."

He and Glencarlyn went into the kitchen together.

Anne's green eyes followed Glencarlyn, lingered on his broad shoulders.

James said, "Anne, what do you say to a trip into the city?"

"What for?"

"For some music, some dancing."

"Dancing?" she grinned. "I've done enough of that in my life. I don't need any more."

"Didn't you like it?" I asked.

James cut in, "Okay then. No dancing. Just to go out, see some bright lights, some new faces."

Her green eyes were fastened on the kitchen door. "Maybe some time, James."

He glanced at me, then lowered his voice. "It would be nice to get away for a little while, wouldn't it?"

"Maybe some time," she repeated.

I knew that she didn't want to leave because of Glencarlyn. As long as he was here, she would stay.

James knew it, too. His mouth tightened. He veiled his gray eyes and plucked at his tie. "He'll be moving on soon," James said quietly. "Just wait and see. He'll be moving on. He's not the kind to hang out around trouble. And we've had plenty of it. When he does move on, he'll go alone."

Anne gave James a hard stare. She didn't answer him.

But I thought that James was wrong about one thing. Glencarlyn wasn't a man to back away from trouble. Whatever my suspicions were, I sensed that much about him.

Barney came in, carrying a loaded tray.

He passed the drinks around. When he gave me my glass, he said, "A light one, just for you, Mary Ellen. So be a good girl and drink it. You need to relax."

I sipped it cautiously. It was tart. Quinine water and something else. I didn't know just what.

Glencarlyn brought in a load of logs, set them down near the fireplace.

For a little while, we talked about the weather, what winter would be like on Point Janeway, what we might need to order in for our comfort.

Glencarlyn leaned at the mantel and said nothing.

Anne went to stand beside him. He seemed not to notice.

I had the feeling that all of us were still thinking of Hester, thinking of her, but carefully not mentioning her name.

I finally couldn't stand it any longer. I excused myself and went up to my room.

I tried to settle down with a book, but found myself dozing over it, dropping off, then suddenly jerking awake.

I heard the others come upstairs. Heard

voices, and footsteps. At last there was silence.

The house was still. An occasional leaf whispered along the roof.

I tried to read, but the print blurred before my eyes. My head dropped. I was so tired . . . so tired. . . . The thought of the effort required to go to bed was too much. I slid deeper into my chair, and the light faded away. . . .

"Mary Ellen, Mary Ellen."

I heard the whisper, the faint sound outside my door.

"Mary Ellen."

I came awake, but very groggy. My head hurt. My throat felt sour. I stumbled to my feet.

"Mary Ellen. . . ."

12

I STUMBLED across the room and eased the door open on a thick curtain of shadow and silence.

I steadied myself, straining to hear the voice again. Had it been real? Or had I dreamed it?

"Mary Ellen."

It was an unrecognizable whisper, this time from further away.

Something dark shifted at the head of the stairway to the kitchen.

Be careful, Glencarlyn had said. *Be very careful, Mary Ellen.*

Had he been warning me of this moment?

Had he known then, in the boulders near the quarry, that this whisper would come to me?

I hesitated. It was thus that Sally had been lured from her room, and Timothy, too. . . .

The shadows shifted again.

I went toward them.

A step creaked suddenly. I heard the faint sound of clothing as it brushed the wall. I heard a whisper of breath.

"Mary Ellen . . ."

It was still further away, drawing me on, on into the darkness.

I was dizzy, swaying at the top of the stairs. I tried to brace myself and took a single step down.

The dark spun around me.

I was off balance suddenly, my footing gone.

I tipped forward, fighting empty air, and fell. . . .

There was pain first. Then there were voices.

Glencarlyn was saying in a deep hard voice, "Mary Ellen, what happened? Are you all right?"

I felt his hand on my cheek, my head. It was warmth, comfort, safety.

And then I remembered.

There had been a voice whispering, "Mary Ellen, Mary Ellen," a voice in the dark that had called to me, drawn me out into the hallway, and then to the stairs.

I kept my eyes closed.

"Mary Ellen," Glencarlyn said, "are you all right? Can you hear me?"

Was it his voice that I had heard?

Was it he who had called me out into the hallway?

I opened my eyes.

He was kneeling beside me, staring down, his blue eyes narrow, cold, not alight with amusement, not faintly smiling. Cold eyes, empty eyes.

Beyond him, I saw Anne, and Barney, and James, huddling together. Their faces were pale. They were utterly silent, unmoving.

I said, struggling to sit up, "I'm okay, I think," and heard Glencarlyn's breath go out in a relieved sigh.

"Would you mind telling me what you were doing?" Anne demanded, her husky voice suddenly shrill. "You very nearly scared me out of my mind, Mary Ellen. I heard that terrible racket, and I thought. . . ." She stopped, bit her lip. "What were you doing?"

But I didn't want to explain. No one must know but me. No one, except me— and the person who had called to me.

"It's pretty late for wandering around, isn't it?" James asked.

"I was thirsty. I wanted a drink of water," I said lamely.

"That vodka and tonic I gave you," Barney laughed. "You poor chick, you don't have a head for the stuff, do you? A couple of sips and you're dehydrated and dizzy, and off you go to fall down the steps."

I had been dizzy, but I hadn't just fallen. I had been called into the hall. And at the top of the steps. . . .

I got to my feet, achingly aware of fresh bruises. I made my way up the staircase.

Glencarlyn came with me.

I stopped at the top.

The step was broken, splintered. When I had put my weight on it in the dark, it had given way.

Glencarlyn made a wordless exclamation as he ran his fingers over the raw wood.

"But what's going on?" Barney asked, looking up at us, and starting up the staircase with Anne and James reluctantly following him.

"It's broken," Glencarlyn said expressionlessly.

Barney groaned, "Oh, man, not again. We got it all fixed up after we moved in. I could swear it ought to have held for ten years."

"It didn't," Glencarlyn answered.

"Craziest thing." Barney shrugged. "Oh, well. I'll do it again in the morning." He scratched his beard, yawned. "Sure you're okay, Mary Ellen?"

I nodded. Had it been his voice that I had heard? Had he stood outside my door and called to me, and then, when I had come out, had he retreated down the steps into the kitchen, and then rushed through to the front staircase and silently made his way to the second floor again? Had he been the one who had drawn me out to the broken step in the dark?

He yawned again, turned toward his room.

"Can I do anything for you?" Anne asked.

"I'm all right. I'll go back to bed," I told her.

"Then good night, Mary Ellen," she said, and disappeared down the hall. When her door closed behind her, the sound of the key turning in the lock was

207

very loud. I wondered then if her husky voice could have produced the sexless whisper I remembered.

James said, "You'd better be careful, Mary Ellen. This is an old house. Anything can happen, it looks like."

Glencarlyn had warned me to be careful.

Now James was doing the same.

But I already knew my danger.

The step had been tampered with. I had been lured into the dark deliberately.

I knew who was next now.

Glencarlyn's arm was around my shoulder. He led me to my room. He stood in the doorway, looking around.

"You were reading." he said finally. "The lamp is on. There's a book on the floor."

"Reading and dozing, I guess."

"Why did you really decide to go downstairs?"

"I told you, didn't I? I got thirsty. I wanted some water."

"There's a sink in the bathroom at the end of the hall," he said dryly.

"I forgot about it."

"Did you?" He stared down at me.

208

"Mary Ellen, I think it's about time that you faced the truth."

I had faced the truth.

But how could I reveal it to him?

I didn't answer.

I went into my room, but I couldn't close the door because he stood in the way, straddling the threshold.

"I'm tired," I said, "and a little dizzy. I ache all over. I don't know what you're talking about, but I want to go to bed."

He smiled faintly. He came in, closed the door behind him.

I opened my mouth to protest.

He said, "Mary Ellen, nothing's going to happen to you. Not now. And I've got to talk to you."

"But I . . ."

"All right. You feel terrible. It could be worse. A lot worse."

I sank down on the edge of the bed.

He stood over me.

"It's time for you to leave here," he said quietly. "That's the truth I want you to face."

Sally . . . Timothy . . . Hester. . . .

And now me.

I had managed to escape this time. But what about the next?

"Don't you see what's happening?" Glencarlyn asked.

What was happening?

Gentry Carrier had brought the seven of us together at Point Janeway, saying we were Ralph Dartmoor's heirs. And then the lawyer had disappeared. But the house had been sold only months before although Ralph Dartmoor had been dead for four years. *He never did you a favor*, Josh Renner had said, referring to the man I had thought my benefactor. Josh Renner had been right. The seven of us had been brought here for some purpose.

Were we legitimate heirs? And had one of us, more greedy than the rest, determined to destroy us to have the money and Point Janeway for himself?

Or was the pattern I had seen emerging the real reason? Was there a madman loose on Point Janeway, a madman punishing each of the heirs for the sins in their pasts?

Sally, Timothy, Hester. . . .

Then why had I been next?

What lay hidden behind the menace that had reached for me through the dark?

As if in answer, I heard Carlotta's hysterical words, "You did it. I don't know how, but you did it!" and I saw the small pink pillow on the tangled velvet throw.

The memory of her words shuddered through me. I could hear her strident voice again, see her wild face, her clawed hands reaching for me.

She had accused me of killing Kelly Galligher. Her husband led her away. Afterwards he'd apologized, offered me a bonus, suggested that I leave town. I had refused the bonus, stayed on hunting for work I didn't find.

I knew I had done nothing. I had loved Kelly Galligher, and missed him still. I was sure that I always would. But there was that in my past. Carlotta's accusation. . . .

Like the others, I had something to hide.

That was why I was next.

Glencarlyn was still standing over me. He said, "You understand, don't you?"

I understood, but I said, "I don't know what to do."

"Then let me tell you," he said briskly.

"You just pack your bags. Tomorrow morning, first thing, I'll drive you into the city. You can stay with Mrs. George."

I looked at him, thinking of the gibberish he had typed while pretending that he was a writer. I wondered how he had known about Mrs. George.

I asked quickly, "What about Mrs. George?"

"I said you could stay with her, couldn't you? You'd be safe with her until you settled somewhere else."

"How do you know about her?"

He was silent for a moment, then he grinned, "I've heard you mention her, Mary Ellen. How else would I have learned her name."

"I don't know," I said slowly. It was possible, of course. The others knew about Mrs. George, knew I wrote to her, heard from her, knew I had visited her once. Glencarlyn could have, too.

"That's not here or there," he said. "Stay wherever you want. If you don't have the money, I'll stake you, and you can pay me back when you want to."

"Why?" I demanded.

"Because I think you should get out of here."

"But why?" I pressed.

He said grimly, "Because, like the state police, I think something is wrong. One suicide, two accidents, in so short a time. . . ."

I drew a deep careful breath. A wave of dizziness washed over me. I struggled against it while Glencarlyn's face seemed to fade momentarily into mists. I shook my head to clear it. I had to think. I had to plan.

At last I said, "What do you think happened to Sally? To the others?"

He didn't answer me.

"And to me, tonight?" I went on in a whisper.

"I don't know," he said after a long silent moment.

"You don't think the step broke under my weight, do you?"

"Do you?" he asked finally.

"No."

There was so much more to say, to tell him. The whisper from the dark, the moving shadow . . . I didn't dare.

He said, "That's why you must leave as

213

soon as you can. That's what I wanted you to understand."

Leaving meant escape, but it also meant never knowing the truth. It meant fear for the rest of my life.

And staying meant ever-present danger, and possibly death.

I couldn't think now. Not with the dizziness sweeping over me again. Not with my head aching.

"I'll decide in the morning," I said.

"You have to decide to go," he urged. "You have to do it now."

But I asked myself how I could trust him.

He went to the door, opened it. He peered into the hallway, looking both ways, and then closed the door again.

He came back to stand over me. "Mary Ellen, you said you were dizzy before, and I can see that you still are. You said you were dozing just before you went into the hall." He stared into my eyes. "Why did you do that?"

I shrugged.

"Something made you go out there. And it wasn't just thirst."

"I might have . . . well, maybe I heard something. I'm not sure. I just . . ."

He cut in, "I think you've been drugged."

"Drugged?" I echoed.

"The pupils of your eyes are quite enlarged. You had a drink earlier, remember?"

I remembered. But I also remembered that Barney and Glencarlyn had gone into the kitchen together. Glencarlyn had stepped out for firewood, and Barney had carried in the drinks, handed me mine.

Either he or Glencarlyn could have put something into my glass. And either he, or Glencarlyn, could have called to me from the dark.

Then why would Glencarlyn mention that possibility to me? Why would he warn me of a danger with which he himself was threatening me?

"It could come from any direction," Glencarlyn said. "Any time. Any way. You must understand that, Mary Ellen. You won't be safe until you're gone from here."

The warning could be just one part of his urging me to leave Point Janeway. Was he intent on that because he was trying to help me? Was he as sure as I that I was next on a madman's murder list? Or did Glencarlyn have his own reasons for what he said?

Tiredness crept through my aching body. I had been frightened for too long. I had been struggling against terror for too long. It seemed then that I could bear it no longer.

Whatever Glencarlyn's motives, he was right. I had to get away. I mustn't allow myself to think of Sally, and Timothy, and Hester. I must escape from the net that hovered over me.

I said, "I'll be ready to leave in the morning."

He nodded, said good night, and left me, closing the door carefully behind him.

As his footsteps faded away down the hall, I carefully turned the key in the lock.

My sleep was dream-haunted. I swayed dizzily at the top of the dark stairs, while a voice called my name from the shadows. I saw Hester tumbling from the rim of the quarry. I heard drum rolls of thunder while Timothy's plump body hurtled from the stony path to the boulders below. I saw Sally's pink face fade into a small pink pillow.

I awakened early, glad of escape from the torment of the night, only to face the terrors of the day.

I knew that Glencarlyn was right, whatever his reasons. I had to go away. I had to go away, I told myself uneasily, as I dressed, as I stepped carefully over the broken riser on my way down to the kitchen.

It wouldn't take me long to pack, I thought uneasily. I would just have coffee first, and then tell the others. Within an hour or two I would be gone from Point Janeway for good.

We were at the kitchen table.

A cold mist seemed to be seeping through the windows.

I heard the sound of the axe from outside, and knew that Barney must be cutting more firewood.

James' hand shook as he put down his mug of coffee. He said slowly, "But Mary Ellen, why? Why should you leave?"

"I just don't want to stay any more," I told him, my voice strange-sounding in my ears. "And I think that the rest of you should leave, too."

"That's easier said than done," he said quietly, his thin face shrinking under his sandy hair.

"But you could go back to your job, couldn't you?"

He shook his head.

"Why not, James?"

He was quiet for a long time. Then, with a despairing sigh, he said, "I had some trouble at the bank. I promised to get it straightened out. And I will. I will, I tell you. I'll pay back every cent. That's what I use the monthly check for. But it leaves me next to nothing. If I move away, I'm lost." He raised his gray eyes, "And then, there's Anne. I don't want to be separated from her."

The mist at the windows seemed to swirl around me. The pattern was completely clear now. Each one of us had had something to hide. Each of the seven of us had pasts we wanted to forget. And one of us was determined to destroy the rest. If it were not accomplished here in Point Janeway, would he continue? Would he track us down, follow us forever?

Anne stood laughing in the doorway. "Who's taking my name in vain?"

James managed a tight smile. "Nobody. And listen, you'd better see what you can do. Mary Ellen's talking about pulling out today."

"Pulling out," Anne cried. "Oh, but you can't." She dropped into a chair, doubled her fists under her chin. "If you do, then what about me? I can't stay here all by myself. Not with just Barney and James. I'd go crazy. I just couldn't. . . ."

"Glencarlyn would be here," I told her softly.

"Oh, yes. Maybe. But maybe he wouldn't either."

Glencarlyn had said he would drive me to the city. He didn't say he would be staying there. He didn't say that he would not be either. I wondered which was the truth. Then I wondered what might happen to me on the drive in.

I looked at Anne. "Why don't you come with me? We can figure out something."

She hesitated briefly. Then, "I can't, Mary Ellen. I have my reasons for staying. Just as you have your reasons for wanting to go." She slanted an anxious green look at me. "I couldn't give up my share of the house. I need it. I have to have it."

"It seems," Barney said, lounging in the doorway, "as if there's lots of heat in this cold kitchen."

"Mary Ellen's going!" Anne cried.

He stared at me, a grin spreading within his black beard. "Hey, what's with you? I never figured you for such a scary type. I mean, it's enough to blow your mind, sure, the step breaking, all that. But we've got to stick together, you know. It's the four of us now. Just the four of us. We can't break it up and lose everything, can we?"

13

THE three of them watched me, each one urgent and pleading. It was obvious that they were desperate for me to remain with them.

Was it because, in Barney's words, "We have to stick together?"

Did Anne really feel that she couldn't stay on without me?

How could my leaving affect James, whose newly-confessed embezzlement completed the pattern and raised fresh questions in my mind?

All of the seven brought together in Point Janeway, the four of us here in the gloomy kitchen now, the three buried in the quiet Stony Ridge cemetery, were of roughly the same age, alone in the world and, most important of all, we had turned our backs on memories we couldn't bear.

I had thought, at first, that perhaps one of us had reached in greed for all the money, for full ownership of the house. And later, seeing that we had been brought together for some purpose, I had thought a madman among us had set out to punish each of us for our individual sins.

But the punishment of death was out of proportion to our crimes. Even a madman would understand Timothy's hungry-hearted and sad lies, and Sally's single, and paid for, theft.

If they had been murdered, not out of a madman's compulsion, but as part of a carefully conceived plan to obliterate us all, then the deaths of all must be to hide the death of one. A small black shadow had reached from the past to destroy only one of us, and had covered us all.

Who hid behind that shadow?

Was he one of the three remaining? Anne? James? Barney?

Or was he the only outsider? Glencarlyn?

Now Anne said quietly, her green eyes on my face, "All right, Mary Ellen. Maybe you have some real reason for wanting to desert us. But if you do, I think you have to tell us what it is."

"Yes," agreed James. "I say the same."

But I couldn't tell them the truth. I was

afraid to say the word murder. I feared the reaching dark shadow. I knew I was next. To escape, I must run away. And then, uneasily, I asked myself if the escape from Point Janeway would really free me. Would I be able to forget the reaching hand? Or would it pursue me forever?

Barney leaned back, grinned in his beard. "What I think is, you chicks ought to fight it out between you. You're both big girls, over twenty-one. And both good-looking. It's an equal match."

Anne flashed him a hostile green look, and James' thin face tightened.

"There's nothing to fight about," I told him. "That's not why . . ."

"Come on, Mary Ellen. Who do you think you're kidding?" he snorted. "You're just running away from it. Why not come out and say so. After all, you're among friends."

Running away. . . . Yes. Yes, I was. Why did he, the others, play this game of pretense? Surely Sally and Hester and Timothy were in their minds. Surely they remembered my fall the night before.

I said slowly, "The house isn't worth it to me, I guess."

Barney laughed aloud, "Quiet Mary Ellen, I'm not talking about the house." His pale blue eyes went past my shoulder.

I turned, the movement reminding me of my bruises. I instantly forgot them.

For Glencarlyn was standing in the doorway, unabashedly listening, his face expressionless.

Anne grinned at him.

James plucked the crease in his trousers.

Barney gave him a small welcoming salute.

Glencarlyn asked, "Are you packed, Mary Ellen?"

I shook my head. I looked from Barney, to Anne, to James.

It might be that unknowingly all three of them stood under the sentence of death, along with me. It might be that only two of them did.

I thought of Mrs. George's small cottage, and my room there. How pleasant it would be to retreat to its safety, to hide away, to escape the danger that hung over me. I could pretend to myself that I had never received the letter from Gentry Carrier, that I had never met the others, joined them in this venture. But Sally, and

Timothy, and Hester were dead. I couldn't pretend that they were still alive, could I?

I couldn't wipe out three murders.

I couldn't allow a madman to destroy us all.

"Well?" Glencarlyn asked. "What do we do now?"

"I've decided that I won't leave. Not just yet," I said.

Barney grinned. "Brave girl."

I wondered if he meant I had courage to face whatever might happen to me. Or if he was thinking of what he insisted was my rivalry with Anne over Glencarlyn. Let Barney believe that, if he chose. Though I knew better, I thought. The less he, the others, suspected my real motives, the safer I would be.

Glencarlyn sighed, said with a faint smile, "You're stubborn, Mary Ellen."

Anne gave me a relieved look, but there was a certain hard note in her voice when she said, "That makes me feel better. But I never really thought you'd do it anyhow."

James looked at me sideways, and I knew he was thinking of what he had told me earlier. He would have felt safer had he known that each one of us had something to hide just as painful as he did. But I knew that I would not tell him that.

Barney, suddenly thoughtful, sober, looked at Glencarlyn, "So you were behind it. You suggested it."

Glencarlyn shrugged.

"How come?"

I was startled by how he sounded. It wasn't the words that he spoke. They were just words. But he sounded different. The rhythm, even the voice he used, was unfamiliar.

Glencarlyn answered, "I don't like houses with broken staircases, I guess."

James asked, "Does that mean you're leaving?"

Glencarlyn replied with a question. "Do you want me to?"

James shrugged his thin shoulders, gray eyes going to Anne.

She said quickly, "I don't see why you should."

And Barney, sounding like himself again, said, "Hey, man, we've still got to fix up the road. You said you'd help me with it. Just James and me . . . well, I don't see how we could do it."

Glencarlyn grinned. "I never even thought of moving out."

Soon after, Barney's pounding hammer echoed through the house as he repaired the broken step from which I had hurtled, drugged and dizzy, into the dark.

Two days passed without incident.

A stillness had descended on Point Janeway.

A caution, unspoken but real, had enwrapped all of us.

I watched James and Barney and Anne. I watched Glencarlyn.

And I knew with a deep intuitive certainty that they watched me. They were as much aware of danger as I was. But they continued to play at pretense, masking their fears.

We lived within a net of suspicion, breaths virtually suspended, lives suspended, too, while we waited for something to happen.

No one spoke of those who lay in the Stony Ridge cemetery. No one remarked on the increased size of the checks that arrived on the first day of the month.

Anne and Glencarlyn walked together,

and played cards, and James watched angrily, eyes narrowed and hands nervously plucking the crease in his trousers.

Barney checked and rechecked the road, and made lists of what he needed to repair it, consulting occasionally with the other two men.

There were just the four of us left. And there was the tall, blue-eyed man who had arrived suddenly just before the terror began.

He tapped out gibberish on his typewriter, acting the part of a writer.

He had deliberately sought us out, not come upon us by chance.

He questioned, and pried, in never-ending curiosity.

Who was he? Where had he come from? Why was he here?

Was it he who had brought us together to destroy us?

Something within me rejected those terrible queries. My mind whispered them. Thought gave them words. My heart refused them. Emotions said no. I kept remembering his touch, the sense of safety I had had in his arms. I kept remembering the straightness of his blue gaze, and the faint smile that touched his mouth. But I knew that I mustn't allow myself to be deceived. My life, the lives of all of us left, depended upon what I could make of my suspicions. Where they would lead me. What proof I would find.

And what of James? If he had embezzled from the bank in which he had worked, could he be so greedy that he now wanted all of what Ralph Dartmoor had left? And to own the house completely?

Anne . . . she, too, had shown greed, hunger for money beyond the normal, a willingness to involve herself in an immoral scheme to obtain it. Could a woman have somehow made Sally commit suicide? Could she have tripped Timothy and thrown him on the rocks? Could she have pushed Hester into the quarry?

Barney . . . the draft evader on the run. Did he feel that having all the inheritance would protect him?

Or was greed not really the motive? Was I right when I thought we must all be slated to die for some other, more hidden, reason?

The questions hounded and harried me.

The bruises from my fall faded slowly. But the pressure of uncertainty grew stronger. At last I felt that I had to escape it, at least for a little while.

It was late afternoon, a gray sunless day.

I bundled up in a heavy jacket, put on boots. Before I tied on my head scarf, I fastened the tiny pearl drops Kelly had given me to my ears. They were a symbol to me, a talisman of courage. I had worn them when I first went to see Gentry Carrier.

As I passed Glencarlyn's door I heard the tap of the typewriter. The keys clicked, then stopped.

He came out of his room, asked, "Where are you going?"

"To town," I told him.

"Okay. I'll drive you," he offered.

"But I just want to walk."

He hesitated. Then, "Are you sure? It looks pretty cold out there to me."

"I'm sure." I turned away quickly, not wanting to give him time to offer to go with me, not wanting to have to refuse his company. I wanted to be alone.

He didn't offer. He said, "I guess I'll get back to work."

I nodded, went down the steps, carefully holding the handrail.

Anne was in the living room, I noticed, sewing under the lamp. I wondered what high-fashion outfit she would be wearing at dinner that evening for Glencarlyn's benefit.

James was playing solitaire at the coffee table near her.

There was the sound of the axe from out behind the kitchen, so I knew that Barney must be cutting more firewood.

I left the house, walked carefully along the road, skipping the potholes, edged around the washed-out places.

It took me about fifteen minutes, walking quickly, to reach Stony Ridge.

Dim lights glowed from the Renners' windows, offering the promise of warmth against the gray mist of the afternoon, the promise of warmth and of welcome.

I went in, and the warmth was there, but no welcome.

Josh greeted me with his usual reserve.

Asa grumbled behind his mail table.

Martha peered at me suspiciously around the brown curtain.

It was an unconsidered impulse that

made me ask, "Mrs. Renner, is there someone in Stony Ridge that could trim my hair for me?"

She said stiffly, "You don't want to cut your hair. It's too pretty."

I slipped off the head scarf. "Not cut it. Just take an inch off the ends. That keeps it healthy, I think."

"In the county seat, forty miles . . ." she began.

It was another unconsidered impulse that made me ask, "Could you do me the favor?"

She looked uncertainly from Josh to Asa, then her mouth turned in a smile. "I've been doing my husband's hair all these years. I expect I can do yours, too." She thrust the brown curtain aside. "Come in, and I'll give it a try."

I went into a room that reminded me so strongly of Mrs. George's kitchen I felt instantly at home.

Pots gleamed in a row on the wall near the stove.

A hooked rug was on the floor.

Plants lined the two windows.

My face must have expressed my pleasure, my homesickness, too.

Martha said, "We don't have much, but you don't need much to live nice."

"You sound like a friend of mine, Mrs. George. It's just what she would say. And she proves it, too, the same as you."

"Mrs. George?" Martha cocked her head. "That's who you get your letters from, isn't it?"

I smiled faintly, nodded.

Martha wasn't ashamed to admit that she checked the mail as Asa sorted it.

She looked only slightly discomfited, explaining, "Not much goes on in Stony Ridge. We get interested, you see."

"Of course," I agreed. "That's how it always is in a small town."

She eyed me up and down, then said, "You have a gaunt and bluish look," and asked doubtfully, "Would you like a cup of tea?"

Like Mrs. George again. I found myself grinning. "Oh, yes, I really would," I told her.

She grinned back, all narrow-eyed suspicion gone from her face. "Then sit down. We've plenty of time to get to your hair."

She filled the kettle, set it on the stove,

with a gesture that again reminded me of Mrs. George.

"You know," she said, "it's not just natural nosiness that get's us interested in what goes on around here."

I snuggled comfortably in the padded chair. I felt better, more at ease, safer, than I had felt for days.

She went on, "We're a suspicious lot. Clannish, too. Mountain people always are."

"I guess they have their reasons," I said, wondering what she was leading up to.

She brought out cups and saucers, and a dish piled high with home-made cookies. She set them down, and leaned at the table, repeating, "Yes. I guess they do. Especially . . ." she shot me a quick look, ". . . especially," she went on, "just now."

"Now?" I asked.

"We all knew Ralph Dartmoor, you see. We all knew he was the last, the very last of his line. But really. No question of that. We knew his unmarried sister all her life, and his unmarried brother. We attended their funerals, and the funerals of everyone in that family. And we buried old Ralph

Dartmoor ourselves. So we knew. We knew, child. He had no heirs. The house stood rotting there for four years because he had no heirs. And then you turned up, the bunch of you. Saying you'd inherited the place. The checks from the bank coming each month. His place, and his money. Only there was no money. I can show you the food bills for what Ralph ate, all unpaid, and all always will be. His little pension stopped when he died. He had no money to leave." She smiled faintly. "So what were we to think, child? The lot of you strangers, lowlanders from the city to boot. A queer bunch, and no mistake. That one with the black beard and earring . . . he never comes in here. Those two girls, God rest their souls, with nothing good to say to anybody, with eyes that never looked. That skinny, shifty-eyed boy. The poor plump one with glasses. And then, child, then there's yourself."

I didn't know what to answer.

Her eyes searched my face. She waited.

There had been no money. But the checks came every month from the bank, checks supposedly drawn on an estate left by Ralph Dartmoor, who had had nothing to leave. Now I knew why Gentry Carrier had disappeared. Once we had been gathered at Point Janeway, the trust established, his chore was done. But who had bought the house so recently? And who had set up the false trust? The motive—to get the seven of us together—was clear. The hand behind it was still invisible.

Martha was waiting, her eyes on my face. I said, "I can see how you'd feel."

"You can see why we'd be waiting, and watching, can't you?"

"And then, the deaths. . . ."

She looked relieved. She smiled at me. The kettle came to a boil and she turned quickly to fill the pot.

Her routine, I saw, was the same as Mrs. George's. Two elderly ladies, both making their tea with the same pleasurable ritual. It somehow gave me a good feeling. It was a symbol of continuity. Some day I, too, would make my tea that way. My heart gave a sudden hard thump. But *only if I lived.* . . .

When she had served me, and herself, she sat down. She said, "So we watched. Yes. I admit it. And the tall one with the dark hair came. The one you said wasn't a cousin. All right. But, child, what kind of a man is that? A grown man that doesn't work. The rest of you, a queer enough bunch. But a man that looks like he does, and doesn't work, well. . . ." She shook her head. "We watched harder, knowing what we did. The letters . . . nothing came. Resident advertisements, a few bills for conveniences. The checks from the bank. But nobody, nobody ever got a letter from home, from his folks. Nobody but you."

I could at least gratify her curiosity on that one point. I wanted to. I said, "Mrs. George is the lady I lived with before I came here. She's in her seventies. She . . ."

"You have a friend in her seventies?"

I smiled. "Of course. Why not?"

"With all the talk of a generation gap," Martha said tartly, "this old soul finds that surprising. You're not more than twenty-two, are you?"

"Just twenty-two," I agreed. "Yes. But that has nothing to do with it."

She smiled at me. "Mrs. George. In her seventies. She would be cross with me, I think."

"But why?"

A small astonishing giggle escaped Martha. "I pictured her as a young flibbertigibbet, a city girl, maybe a divorcee even, with nothing to do with her time."

I laughed. "I doubt she'd be cross with you. She'd probably think it funny."

We had finished our tea by then. Martha offered me one more cookie, and when I refused it, she cleared the table.

Then she gave me newspapers to put around my chair, and got her scissors.

Soon she was trimming away.

With each snip of the shears, I thought, there was no money. We had been brought to Point Janeway for a purpose. Three of us had died. And I was next. I was next. . . .

Then Martha said in a thin careful voice, "Don't stay there, child. Not in that house. No good can come of it. I don't know why. I can't give you a reason. But nothing good can come of it."

I felt the cold of the shears against the back of my neck. I felt the sudden unsteadiness of her hand.

I said, "I won't stay longer than I have to."

"Than you have to?"

But I couldn't explain. I didn't dare burden the old lady who stood over me with the fear I could hardly manage myself.

"It won't be much longer," I said at last.

She finished trimming my hair.

I helped her gather the papers and put them away. I thanked her for the tea, and the talk, and the neat job she had done.

She went with me into the front room.

Josh looked at me over his glasses, and smiled.

Asa grumbled.

Martha said defiantly, "I told her. She's a good child, and she listens. So I told her." And she added to me, "Be careful, Mary Ellen. There's doom in Ralph Dartmoor's house."

Doom in Ralph Dartmoor's house. . . .

I remembered her words as I left Stony Ridge behind me, followed the turn-off for the gray stone pillars and what lay beyond it.

The sky was darkening with an early

twilight, with the gray, low-hanging clouds characteristic of late autumn.

The chill air held a dampness that seemed to sink through my flesh to frost the marrow of my bones. A slow steady wind hummed in the bare limbs of the warped trees, and sent crusty leaves underfoot scurrying away from me.

There was an ever-present whisper of sound around me, the whisper of wind and leaves, my own cautious footsteps, but beneath it, underscoring it, there was a deep silence. The silence of vast distances and emptiness. I could hear my pulse beat in my ears, my breath pass my lips.

I moved carefully, stepping across the potholes when I could, circling them when they were too large and deep. I watched ahead for the washed-out places.

I rounded a small curve, and stopped suddenly. A log lay across the road. I wondered how it had come there when it hadn't been there when I passed that way earlier.

I went around it warily, forced off the broken road and into the deep, hardly penetrable brush.

I took one careful step, then another.

It was shadowed here, dark, even though faint light still glowed through the clouds overhead.

Something caught in my jacket, and I stumbled, trying to pull free.

I heard a quick panting breath, a movement behind me. Arms, hot and strong, encircled me, crushed me, forced me forward. I struggled, flung back my head.

Something brushed my cheek, leaving a peculiar tingle behind.

There was a shout from the distance, a crashing in the brush.

I was suddenly free, falling.

I heard a clatter of metal, a strange and unfamiliar sound, a frightening sound.

I heard it, and was swept suddenly aside, falling still, but away from the source of that spine-chilling noise.

I landed hard, the breath knocked out of me, with the gray sky suddenly swooping down.

14

I WAS stunned, shocked into immobility.

A strange numbness enshrouded me.

It lasted for only a moment.

Then I felt the first waves of bruising pain. My back, my legs, my arms stung and ached. New bruises on old ones. I pushed myself up slowly, groping for full consciousness, for memory, for the recollection of some important detail. . . .

I had been circling the log, been forced off the road and into the deep brush. I had stumbled. Arms caught me, thrust me forward, suddenly let me go. The metal clatter echoed in the silence as I fell, my body hurled aside. Arms had caught me, crushed me, shoved me forward. I'd felt a tingling at my cheek. A familiar tingling. . . . Fur. Hair. I suddenly remembered the shadowy lounge where we had decided we would live together.

242

Barney kissing my wrist, his beard tingling on my skin. Barney!

I pushed myself up. My lips went dry, my throat tight. I had not escaped after all, I realized with terror.

Glencarlyn knelt in the shadows a step away from me. He was motionless, staring into the brush.

A small frightened sound passed my lips.

He turned, looked at me, his face rigid. "Who was it?" he demanded.

I scrambled to my feet, backed away.

Glencarlyn, here, alone in the brush. . . .

He rose, took a step toward me.

Again I edged back.

He stopped. "Don't be afraid of me," he said in a harsh voice. "You must know I won't hurt you." Then, "Do you know who it was?"

"I don't . . ."

"Mary Ellen, I followed you from the house to the Renners'." He grinned faintly. "I'll admit that I nearly froze to death, waiting for you to come out. Then I followed you here."

"But why?"

"You know why."

I didn't answer him.

"You were drugged. The step was deliberately broken. I've been watching. And I very nearly didn't make it." He turned, looked at the brush near him. "Do you know what that is?"

My unwilling feet brought me close to him. I studied the black prongs, sharp as knives, the oil-wet hinges.

I remembered the terrible clang of metal. I whispered, "It's the bear trap. It was . . . it was in the shed. I remember."

"The hinges have been oiled recently. You can see that for yourself. You were supposed to fall into it. It's a vicious thing, Mary Ellen."

Again I didn't answer him.

"There was someone here. I know that. I heard him. I had dropped back, hoping you wouldn't know I was around."

I said faintly, "Someone grabbed me. I was pushed forward, then let go. When I fell . . ."

"I hit you pretty hard," Glencarlyn told me.

But was that the truth?

Had Glencarlyn knocked me away from

244

the terrible pronged teeth of the bear trap? Or had it been he who had held me, thrust me toward it?

The tingling sensation at my cheek. The fur. Beard. Barney.

Glencarlyn was watching me. I knew he was waiting. I brushed leaves, bits of broken twigs from my jacket. But I didn't trust him. I didn't tell him that I thought it might have been Barney's arms around me. I thought my only safety was in silence.

Had Barney broken the step, hoping I would fall and die in the dark?

Had he set the bear trap, thinking I would be impaled on its prongs?

Or had that been Glencarlyn himself?

I said lamely, "Thank you for your help."

He asked harshly, "You won't tell me who was here? Who you think it was?"

"I don't know. I'm not sure."

"Then let's go on to the house," he answered.

I didn't want to.

Martha had said there was doom in Ralph Dartmoor's house, and she was right. She was right, as I well knew.

But I followed Glencarlyn back to the log, stumbled along beside him, up the road, and then between the gray stone pillars.

Barney . . . what did I know of him except what he had told me? That he was from California, on the run from the draft. Just that. Nothing more. Why should he hate me? The others? Why should he have gathered us together to destroy us? Was it for the money, the house? Or was it for some other reason? Were we connected, linked, without my knowing it? Was he connected, linked, to one of the others, without their knowing it?

Barney. . . .

I decided I must learn everything that I could about him. I must trap him, taking whatever risk I had to, if possible. I must prove him either innocent, or guilty. If I could prove him innocent, then I would have imagined the tingle of the touch of his beard. I would go on to the others. Test each of them, one by one.

I set out to see what I could learn that evening. I used the only technique I knew.

After dinner, excusing myself from the others, I went for a walk.

Frightened, cold, listening, searching the dark with anxious eyes, I offered myself as bait.

If I was to be the next victim, I would make it easy. I would draw the enemy into the light.

But no one came to me.

Not Barney.

Not James, nor Anne.

And not Glencarlyn, either.

The next morning, when Barney was chopping firewood out back, I ambled outside. I sat on the kitchen steps, watching him.

His long hair blew in the wind. I could not help but see his beard. His watered-ink blue eyes were red-rimmed. But he grinned, "You're a glutton for cold aren't you, quiet Mary Ellen?"

"It's not so bad," I answered. Then, "You don't seem to mind it so much yourself."

"I don't," he agreed. "It keeps my blood working."

"I'd think it would be just the opposite," I observed. "Your being from California, I mean. It ought to make you feel it even more than the rest of us."

There was a brief pause in the rhythm of the rising and falling axe. Had Barney realized what I was doing? Had he realized that I was suspicious of him? That I had recognized those tight arms around me? That I thought he had seized me in the brush, tried to force me to fall into the bear trap?

"Everybody's different," he was saying. He thrust the axe into a log, came and sat beside me. "Are you still thinking about leaving?"

I shook my head.

"A pretty chick like you," he chuckled. "You don't have anything to worry about. You'll make out all right. No matter where you are."

I smiled, pretending thanks for the compliment.

"Especially with money for ballast. Not that you need it. But it helps, doesn't it?"

"I suppose it does."

"Suppose," he mocked me. "Let me tell you, Mary Ellen. I know."

"Then you must have had money once."

"Of course I did. I grew up with it. My family. . . ."

I sat very still, holding my breath.

248

Barney had never spoken of having a family. I had always assumed that he was alone as the rest of us. As for money—his worn boots, the fringed vest, his faded blue jeans hardly implied a background of wealth.

He was looking at me sideways, chuckling, "Listen to me, will you? I'm as bad as Timothy was. My family. It's just a way of talking, of course. But why should I pretend with you? Money is like good strong muscle. With it you can do anything, anything you want to or not to."

"Maybe," I said.

"Money is power," he said. "It can wipe out any threat." And then, laughing suddenly, he got to his feet. He went to where he had left the axe, and hefted it. He swung it quickly.

I found myself cringing as its sharp blade bit into the huge log. For just a second, I had felt his pale eyes on me. I wondered if he had considered me as a target instead of the log. Then I wondered if I had imagined his glance.

I rose, turned to go inside.

That was when I saw Glencarlyn. He was at the window of his room, leaning out through the blowing white curtains, and staring down at me.

I wondered how long he had been there, and what he had heard.

It was later that same day.

I announced that I was walking into Stony Ridge again. I made sure that Barney, that everyone else, knew my plans.

I moved quickly and carefully down the road, alert, listening, watching.

The wind blew through the brush and whispered in the trees, and the crisp leaves danced.

But if anyone followed me, I didn't know it.

I visited with Martha and Josh and Asa, bought a pad and some pencils, and soon started back to the house.

The sun was bright, casting long dark shadows ahead of me. The sky was cloudless.

Listening still, watching still, I heard no one, saw no one.

I knew that if I were to successfully entrap Barney, it would have to be soon. Yet I couldn't see how to do it except as

I was trying to now. I must make myself available for his attack, and hope, pray, that being watchful, I could circumvent his intentions.

A shiver touched me. How could I? Was I taking more of a risk than I could successfully handle?

I knew, I was certain in my bones, that Barney—or if it wasn't Barney, then whomever it was—would attack again, and soon. First the broken step, then the bear trap. Two make-believe accidents had already befallen me. I obviously had been warned. So there must be another one. A fatal one, and quickly.

Either that, or I was wrong, and Anne could be next, or James. If Barney had not reached for me with those threatening arms, then he himself might be the next victim.

I made my way back along the road, watching, listening. I saw no one, heard nothing.

Yet, when I reached the house, Glencarlyn was sitting on the front steps. He was breathing hard. There was a flush on his cheeks, and perspiration on his forehead. His trousers and sweaters were covered with bits of leaves and twigs. He had plainly just come plunging through the woods.

I stood before him, stared very obviously at his heavy chest.

He smiled faintly, "Have a good walk to town?"

"Did you?" I demanded.

He didn't answer me.

"Were you following me again, Glencarlyn?"

He shrugged, remained silent.

"Couldn't you find the right place? The right time?" I cried.

He raised his eyes, narrowed, watchful eyes. "The right time or place for what, Mary Ellen?"

I wished suddenly that I hadn't expressed my suspicion of him. It meant that I had given myself away. If I were wrong about Barney, if Glencarlyn was my secret enemy, then he had been forewarned. But it was too late. I decided to brazen it out. I thrust the pad and pencils I had bought at Renners' into his hand.

"This is for you," I told Glencarlyn.

He accepted the bag, peered into it. His faint smile widened. He sighed, "I can take a hint. You don't think I'm much of a writer, do you?"

"I don't think you're a writer at all," I said hotly. "You've been here all along under false pretenses. I don't know who you are, or what you're after, but I do know that you're a liar."

His smile faded as I spoke. He turned quickly, looked at the closed door behind him, then at the windows. He got to his feet. "Hold it, Mary Ellen."

"Too much has happened," I cried. "Do you really think . . ."

His arms closed around me. He pulled me to him. His lips touched my cheek. "Not here," he whispered. "Not now. Trust me. Don't give me away."

It was a make-believe kiss, a pretense at an embrace. Yet it shook me strangely.

I was frightened. My heart began to beat very hard. At the same time there was a familiar sweetness in his touch, in the feeling of his arms around me.

It could never have been Glencarlyn that seized me in the brush, forced me toward the bear trap. I would have known. I would have been certain.

He stepped back, an arm sliding around

my waist. "Let's take a walk, Mary Ellen. I guess it's time, and maybe over time, that I told you."

For an instant, I hesitated. Where was he going to take me? What did he mean to do? Would he really explain?

"Trust me," he said, looking down at me. "Just this once. For a few minutes. Come with me."

I did. I let him draw me away from the house. Anyone watching from the windows of Point Janeway would have thought we were lovers, I thought, and blushed.

He led me in a wide circle. The ground under my feet became rocky and steep as we cut through the warped black trees. He took me along the path where I had found Timothy's shoe, and I knew then that we were heading for the quarry. For the place where Hester had died.

My body stiffened, my feet dragged.

Glencarlyn's arm tightened at my waist. "We mustn't be overheard," he said. "It's the only place where I can be sure."

Was that what he had in mind? I asked myself.

I knew that I might be taking my life in my hands, offering it to him.

I knew that he might suddenly turn on me.

What I feared might already be planned in his mind, awaiting only its execution, which would be my execution, too.

But I had reached the limit of my endurance. I had to know the truth.

Had Barney brought us together to destroy us?

Or had it been Glencarlyn.

I would know, I told myself. In moments now, I would know.

We reached the rim of the quarry.

Glencarlyn's arm dropped away from me.

He folded his long legs and sat down, gesturing to the place beside him.

"Nobody can get close enough to hear us, not unless I hear him first, Mary Ellen."

I let myself down gingerly, primly tucking my skirt around my legs. I folded my hands in my lap, the fingers gripping each other so tightly that they hurt.

He gave me a faint smile, then sighed,

"You've been taking too many risks, Mary Ellen."

I wondered if this was one of them, if being alone here with him was the last risk I would take.

He went on, "You're trying to get Barney to show his hand, aren't you?"

"I don't know what you mean," I said. "If I want to talk to Barney . . ."

"But you don't," Glencarlyn said softly. "Though that might be what you hope he'll think. I know you better in the first place. In the second, I know something else, too."

"Suppose you tell me," I said coldly.

"I'm going to have to. Although I wish I didn't." His voice roughened. "If you weren't such a little fool, if you'd trust me, I think I could get you out of it safely. But . . ."

"Out of what?" I cried.

He said gently, "Mary Ellen, you've guessed, haven't you? You've known for some time that there wasn't a real inheritance, haven't you?"

My eyes widened. I whispered, "I had begun to suspect. . . . I wasn't sure. Josh Renner told me the house had been bought not long ago, but Ralph had been dead for four years. And Martha said there was never any money. I couldn't see. . . ." I stopped, collected myself. "But how did you know? How did you find out?"

"Probably in the same way that you did, if that's what you mean. Except that I started at a different point."

"You started at a different point?" I repeated.

"In place. And in time." Glencarlyn turned from me, looked past the quarry edge into the fathomless green water so far below. "I'll tell you about that in a minute. But when did you begin to worry about it?"

"The lawyer," I explained. "Gentry Carrier. I . . . I went to see him after we moved to Point Janeway. He was gone, Glencarlyn. As if he'd never existed. But he had, of course. He'd gotten us together, and set up the trust from which our checks were to be paid. Then he was gone. The office was vacant, the phone disconnected."

Glencarlyn nodded. "Why did you go looking for him?"

Why? It was suddenly hard to

understand. What had happened seemed to make it unimportant. I said, "I thought he could tell me more about my family, about how I was related to Ralph Dartmoor."

"You weren't," Glencarlyn said. "None of you were."

"But how do you know?" I asked quickly.

"That's how I started. The point from which I began," he said quietly, his eyes still fixed on the water far below us. "It was just about a year ago that Kelly Galligher came into my office, Mary Ellen. A fine old man, crusty in spite of ill health, but guilt-ridden beyond his endurance by then."

"You knew Kelly?" I gasped.

And I felt the familiar longing, the same sense of irretrievable loss that memory of Kelly always brought me.

Glencarlyn folded his hands into fists on his knees. "You saw through me the first time, Mary Ellen. I am interested in crime, in mysteries. I'm a private detective. And as you guessed, though I'm not sure how, not much of a writer of love stories."

"I looked in your room," I told him.

He frowned. "I've always kept it locked, and the paper I worked on destroyed."

"Except the day Hester was killed," I reminded him, thinking of how I had crept into his room when he raced out to the quarry.

"Yes. That day. A bad one." Glencarlyn shrugged. "We'll get to that later."

"Kelly. . . ."

Glencarlyn turned, looked at me. His blue eyes were alight with force. "Before I say anything more, I want you to promise that you'll stop trying to do what mustn't be your job. I don't want you to risk your life. I want you to leave here."

"And what will happen?" I demanded.

"Nothing."

"Nothing!" I echoed bitterly.

He cut in, "All right. First, just listen. Then you'll understand."

"Kelly," I said again.

"He was old, I said, and guilt-ridden. He was afraid he didn't have much longer to live. And there was something he had to do, and do quickly." Glencarlyn sighed. "He'd had a daughter, you see. An illegitimate daughter, some twenty-one years

259

before. A child born to a young woman who worked for him. But Kelly had a wife in a mental institution. He had a daughter named Carlotta, and a son named Benjamin. He was caught and didn't know what to do. His sweetheart disappeared along with the infant. That was all he knew. He told me what he could, and I set out to find that infant. It took me quite a long time. But I did it."

I knew what he was going to say before he formed the words. I remembered the closeness I'd felt to Kelly. I remembered his gruff affection. I remembered his painful and always unexplained regrets.

"Yes," Glencarlyn said. "I found you."

15

TEARS stung my eyes. My throat tightened.

Kelly had been the father I had never known, one half of the family I had yearned for for years.

Glencarlyn said quietly, "You weren't just deserted in that school when you were three, Mary Ellen. Your mother was in a strange city. She had no friends. She left you there while she worked, and one day, she was killed in a hit-and-run accident. So you ended up in the state home."

I nodded. But my mother was still faceless to me. Kelly was different. He had shown his love for me. It had sheltered me for his last six months on this earth.

Glencarlyn went on, "Once I found you, he wouldn't be content until he'd met you. It seemed like an accidental meeting, but it wasn't, of course. I had followed you for days. I saw you in the park, and hurriedly got Mark Gormley to bring him down.

The rest was up to him, and he managed it well."

"I never dreamed. I hadn't the faintest. . . ."

"That was what he wanted. Just to be with you, see you, in whatever time he had left. It was less than he thought it would be."

"But why?"

"The secrecy? The arranged meeting?"

I nodded.

"Kelly's wife was dead, but there was still Carlotta to be considered. And her husband. Jim Henry wants to be the next governor of the state, Mary Ellen. An illegitimate child in the family would not help."

"Yes," I agreed absently. "It doesn't matter."

I was thinking of Carlotta's animosity to me. Had she known? Guessed? Was that why she had disliked me so? Was the exposure of my illegitimacy so much of a threat to her?

Glencarlyn's voice deepened as he went on. "Kelly died after six months. I heard of it, of course. But he was an old man. It didn't occur to me to ask questions. But many months later I received a letter from Julie, Mark's wife. It sounded odd to me. Julie and Mark had moved to Florida, judging by the postmark, but there was no return address. That was peculiar to begin with. But also she expressed concern about you. She said Jim Henry had offered you a bonus, and you'd refused it. She said Mark hadn't wanted her to write, but she was afraid you were in trouble. I decided to check up for myself. I found you'd moved in with Mrs. George, that you hadn't been able to get another job. In spite of the Henry references. Then I learned it was *because* of them. I talked to two of the women who'd almost hired you. They said they'd spoken to Carlotta. That while she'd not said anything directly against you, she'd sounded odd, reserved, as if she didn't quite trust you. That was what turned them off."

"But why would Carlotta do that?"

He didn't answer my cry. He said, "By the time I had caught up with you, you'd had the letter from Gentry Carrier, and you'd moved up to Point Janeway with the others."

"Then you were the salesman," I

whispered, remembering that Mrs. George had told me a man had been by, asking for me, not long after I left.

Glencarlyn nodded. "I was. And she's a sweet old lady. But lonely, and therefore talkative." He drew a deep breath, went on, "Mary Ellen, I knew everything about you. From who your mother was, to where she had come from. I knew there could be no inheritance from a man named Ralph Dartmoor. And remember, too, after all that, I felt as if I knew you. I couldn't turn my back on what appeared so strange. And there was the letter from Julie, too. I checked up on Gentry Carrier. He had had the office for two weeks. The furniture was rented. I couldn't locate him, but I learned that he was an out-of-work actor, something of a drunk, who'd do anything for money. So . . . well, I finished up some jobs I had to do, and I came up here, planning to use whatever pretext I had to to get into the house and stay." His faint smile showed, then faded. "A little sleight of hand. I wanted to keep an eye on you, so I made it seem that I was attracted to Anne."

"But what about Gentry Carrier—or whatever his name was?"

"That was what made me suspicious. Why a fake inheritance? Why were you all brought together up here? Then Sally committed suicide, supposedly. It didn't ring true. And Timothy's fall—well, he'd hit his head, at the back, but I was sure if he'd really fallen he would have landed on his face or his chest." Glencarlyn shrugged. "And Hester—you know how afraid of the quarry she was."

"You decided there had been three murders," I whispered.

"Yes. But I had no proof. My suspicions couldn't be evidence. I tried to get you to leave here."

I stared at him, my lips dry, my eyes stinging. At last I whispered, "Then I . . . I am the reason for all this?"

He nodded, turned to give the house, the slope, a long careful look. "Yes. I'm sure you are, Mary Ellen."

I had known I was to be next.

I had considered it.

I had recognized it.

But the words were a shock. I didn't understand.

I blurted, "But who? Why?"

Glencarlyn's voice was deep, harsh. "That question takes us back to the Gallighers again, Mary Ellen. You knew that Kelly had a black sheep of a son named Benjamin, didn't you?"

"Julie mentioned him, but she said Kelly wouldn't want me to talk of him."

"Kelly had given up on Benjamin." Glencarlyn took a deep breath. "I think Benjamin Galligher is Barney Gray."

"Barney!"

"You guessed that he had attacked you, didn't you? Isn't that why you were offering yourself as bait to him, particularly to him?"

"It was his beard, you see. That is, I thought I felt his beard. But I wasn't sure. I couldn't accuse him . . ." I stopped myself then. "Glencarlyn, why should Benjamin Galligher hate me so?"

"I don't know that."

"But there's no reason, there's no. . . ."

My voice trailed off. I remembered Carlotta's hysterical accusations, and I remembered how she had run across the terrace when she left Kelly. I remembered how I had found him, the pink pillow on the tangled velvet throw. Carlotta. . . .

Glencarlyn said quietly, "You see it now, don't you?"

"I don't know. I don't know. . . ."

He said remorselessly, "Carlotta accused you of killing Kelly, didn't she? And later, Jim Henry apologized and tried to get you to leave town."

I raised my eyes to his.

"What does that suggest to you, Mary Ellen?"

"They wanted me to go away. But it . . . it was because Jim Henry was sorry for the awful things she said."

"I expect he was," Glencarlyn said dryly. "But not for your sake. For hers, and his, too."

"But Barney, if he is Benjamin, how does he fit in?"

"I don't know how he was brought in to it, Mary Ellen. But he inherited a substantial legacy when Kelly died. I think he arranged for the house to be bought and deposited money in the bank for the supposed inheritance. I believe he got you here to kill you, and killed the others first, to hide the real motive for your murder.

You are the only one that was important to him."

Carlotta. . . . Her white terrified face, shriveling under the pale light of the terrace, the quick patter of her footsteps.

I shivered, living through those moments again.

Her voice accusing me. . . .

Glencarlyn said, "I want you to leave. Now. Tonight, Mary Ellen. Leave Barney, or Benjamin, to me."

I took a deep breath, knowing what I had to do. I said, "I won't do it. I can't."

"Don't you see? He's determined, maybe demented. He won't let go. Whatever his reasons, he . . ."

"That's just it, Glencarlyn. He won't let go. No matter where I am, he'll follow me. And what of the others? Sally, and Timothy, and Hester? They have the right . . . they mustn't be forgotten. I can't run away, pretend. I can't."

"I can't let anything happen to you," he said roughly.

"Then help me," I pleaded. "Help me unmask him. Help me discover the truth. I owe it to the others. I owe it to Kelly, too, Glencarlyn."

He was still, his face hard, his eyes thoughtful.

I said, "If you won't, then I'll do it alone. Somehow, someway, no matter what it takes. I'll prove it."

He sighed. His big hand closed over mine. "All right, Mary Ellen. We'll give it just one more day. Tell them you're leaving in the morning. Pack up so they'll believe it. Be obvious, but not too obvious. And then make sure that Barney has his chance at you. I'll be watching. I'll be waiting."

The house was still, shrouded in darkness.

I lay in my bed, staring into the shadows.

My two packed suitcases were near the unlocked door.

I had told them at dinner that I would leave in the morning.

Anne's pained protest seemed strained. Her green eyes flashed at Glencarlyn, then at James.

James himself sat very still.

Barney just grinned.

We had spent the evening together in the living room, though twice I had gone out to the porch alone, wondering if Barney would follow me. He didn't. No one did.

Now I lay awake, wonderig if Glencarlyn and I had been wrong.

Perhaps it wasn't Barney who was Benjamin Galligher. Perhaps it was James. And perhaps it wasn't I who was the intended victim. Glencarlyn's suspicions about the Gallighers could be nothing. My own awakened memories could be nothing.

But then I remembered the chord of recogition I had felt when I'd first seen Barney, caught a certain angle of his look. I had seen Kelly in him then. Seen Kelly, and not known it. Barney, I knew then, was indeed Benjamin Galligher. And he was linked to none of the others, only to me. I was his intended victim.

I knew that somewhere nearby Glencarlyn would be going over it in his mind, thinking, planning in much the same way that I was doing now.

And then there was a faint scratch of sound. I couldn't identify it.

I strained, listening hard.

I wondered if Glencarlyn had heard it, too. If he was alerted, ready.

The faint scratch came again.

I threw back the quilts, and slipped from my bed. I was still fully clothed. I went to my door, waited again.

Now there was silence, emptiness.

I held my breath.

"Mary Ellen . . . Mary Ellen. . . ."

The hoarse whisper drifted toward me from somewhere down below.

"Mary Ellen. . . ."

I quietly opened the door.

I took a step out into the darkness, and then another.

"Mary Ellen. . . ."

I moved toward the stairs, and then down them, holding on to the handrail, my shoulders rigid with fright.

I didn't know where Glencarlyn was.

I didn't know if he had heard me leave my room.

But I couldn't stop now. I couldn't turn back.

I moved cautiously into the kitchen.

I saw a shadow, heard the intake of a swift breath.

The light flashed on.

271

Barney stood within feet of me, the axe upraised, glinting. The door behind him was open on the night.

The kitchen was a shambles.

Every cannister had been emptied on the floor. Every dish had been taken out of the cupboards.

I stared at the disarray, then at Barney.

He gave me a thin smile, lowering the axe. Glencarlyn said, "It won't work, Benjamin," and dropped his hand from the light switch.

I knew he must have come down the front staircase, moving silently through the foyer to station himself just outside the door.

Barney showed his teeth through his beard. "Benjamin." He took a step backwards, a step closer to the black night behind him.

"We know the truth," Glencarlyn went on quietly. "Carlotta got in touch with you."

"Carlotta, yes." Barney's watered-ink eyes didn't remind me of Kelly then. They reminded me of nothing human. He said, "We both always knew about it." His glance swerved to me. "It was always her.

Her. The old man never cared about anything but her. And then he brought her to the house. Carlotta was wild over it. She couldn't stand it. What about Jim? If people found out. And we'd always hated her anyway, what she stood for. So Carlotta fought with the old man. And that's why it happened. She lost her head, and that pillow was there. . . ."

The pink pillow on the velvet throw. . . .

Kelly's still face.

Carlotta racing away across the terrace, seeing me at the window.

Her accusations. . . .

Now I understood. Sickened, I listened to Barney go on, "So she did it and got scared. That's Carlotta, all right. She accused Mary Ellen, thinking Mary Ellen knew. Jim got Carlotta quieted down. He figured she was just upset. And besides, he couldn't afford any ugly publicity. So he tried to get Mary Ellen out of town by buying her off. But Mary Ellen didn't buy, and didn't leave. Carlotta couldn't let it go. She got in touch with me."

"It's over now," Glencarlyn said.

But Barney—Benjamin—didn't seem to

hear. He couldn't seem to stop talking, explaining. The rhythm of his words had changed, and his voice, too. In spite of the black beard and the gold earring, he seemed different. I realized it was because he had thrown the mask aside.

He chuckled, with froth on his lips, "She was just talking it off, poor Carlotta. But I decided to do something about it. I came into the money, and the rest of it was easy. Fun, even. I came east and got a hold of George Allen—you knew him as Gentry Carrier—an alcoholic actor on the skids. Between us we picked out the five we needed, all at loose ends, all with secrets to hide. Me? Well, poor old Allen was just like everybody else. He saw my hippie uniform, and that's all he saw. So there were seven of us. A lucky number. I bought the house through the mail, set up the trust. And we all ended up here."

I swallowed hard. I leaned against the wall, barely able to stand. I wanted to run away, to hide. But I stood there, listening in horrified fascination as he went on.

"Sally," he said grinning. "She was so naïve. I asked her to meet me in the kitchen. A middle of the night assignation.

She expected. . . ." He shrugged. "Well, you know. I knocked her out, stuck her head in the oven until she was dead, and then dropped her on the floor. Timothy . . . he went up to bed. I went into the kitchen to fix myself a snack, and Glencarlyn came with me. I sent him out for wood, and ran up to Timothy. I told him to meet me a little later on the path because I had something I had to discuss with him. He fell for it. He met me. I knocked him on the head with a rock, and shoved him over the edge."

I shuddered, sick at heart from the casual account of those terrible deeds.

"Hester. Now that was easy. I told her Glencarlyn wanted to meet her at the quarry. Away she danced, shivering in her shoes, but determined not to miss her chance. I was there instead." His blue eyes swerved to me again. "But you, quiet Mary Ellen, you've been a bit of trouble, haven't you? I drugged your drink, and tore up the step and called you down, but you just got a couple of bruises out of it. I got that bear trap set up for you, and you were going right past it so I had to move in and push you into it, and then I heard somebody coming so I had to get away. You missed those prongs by inches. This time was going to be perfect." He gestured around the kitchen with the axe in his hand. "See what I did? It was going to be a prowler. And Mary Ellen interrupted him, scared him. All of it would have been so easy. And the police would have liked it, too. I had it all worked out." He gave me a long hard look. "It's your fault," he cried. "It was always your fault from the beginning."

I didn't know what was going to happen, but Glencarlyn must have.

He launched himself across the room in a low flat dive. His body hurtled into mine, knocking me to the floor.

At the same time the axe spun from Barney's grasp. Its glinting blade flashed through the air in a quick arc. It bit into the wall just where I had been standing only seconds before, and hung there, quivering.

When I had caught my breath, untangled from Glencarlyn, I looked at the doorway. It was empty.

Barney, my half-brother Benjamin, was gone.

I turned blindly into Glencarlyn's welcoming arms.

The state police dragged the quarry. At dawn they found Barney's body.

Frozen in disbelief, Anne and James clung together, standing with Glencarlyn and me, as Barney was wrapped in a rubber sheet, and loaded into an ambulance.

We told the troopers everything we knew, and soon after they left, Glencarlyn and I locked up Point Janeway.

We drove into Stony Ridge for the last time.

Anne and James boarded the bus for the city together, and I was sure I would never see them again.

I went into Renners', Glencarlyn beside me.

Martha smiled, said, "It's all right now, isn't it?" and I knew the mountain grapevine already had told her the whole story.

Asa nodded, and passed me a letter from Mrs. George.

Josh studied me, then Glencarlyn, from over his glasses. "I knew it was wrong," he said. "Ralph Dartmoor never did anybody a favor."

I left the house key with him, for whoever would need it next, and Glencarlyn and I got into his car.

He drew me to his side, smiled faintly. "I've searched for you twice, Mary Ellen. And found you twice, too. But stay good and close. I don't want to have to do it again."

I snuggled against him happily as we left Stony Ridge for good.

THE END

GUIDE
TO THE COLOUR CODING
OF
ULVERSCROFT BOOKS

Many of our readers have written to us expressing their appreciation for the way in which our colour coding has assisted them in selecting the Ulverscroft books of their choice. To remind everyone of our colour coding—this is as follows:

BLACK COVERS
Mysteries

★

BLUE COVERS
Romances

★

RED COVERS
Adventure Suspense and General Fiction

★

ORANGE COVERS
Westerns

★

GREEN COVERS
Non-Fiction